IMPORTANT BILLING AND CREDIT REQUIREMENTS

All producers of *SAFE must* give credit to the Author of the Play in all programs distributed in connection with performances of the Play and in all instances in which the title of the Play appears for purposes of advertising, publicizing or otherwise exploiting the Play and/or a production. The name of the Author *must* appear on a separate line on which no other name appears, immediately following the title, and *must* appear in size of type not less than fifty percent the size of the title type.

In addition, the following credit must appear in all programs distributed in connection with the Work:

(Name of Producer)
presents

"SAFE"
by Tony Glazer and Anthony Ruivivar

SAFE was originally produced by the Imua! Theatre Company, Kaipo Schwab, Artistic Director, Hope Innelli, Managing Director, in association with Broadsword Productions at the Jose Quintero Theatre with the following cast:

FELIZ	Carlin Glynn
SABINA	Yvonne Jung
TRUSS	Jason Wiles
RYAN	Coby Bell
OAKLEY	Henry Afro-Bradley

The production was directed by Anthony Ruivivar; Sets by Antje Ellerman; Lighting by Shawn K. Kaufman; Costumes by Estee Stanley; Fight Choreography by Robert Tuftee; Sound by Mark Bruckner, Stage Manager, Jenna Gottlieb. The first performance was on June 12, 2003.

CHARACTERS

FELIZ............................50's, a Bank Manager

SABINA..................mid 20's, a Bank Teller

TRUSS.......................30's, a Bank Customer

RYAN.........................mid 20's, a Bank Customer

OAKLEY...................mid to late 60's, a Security Officer

TIME

The Present

PLACE

Downtown Manhattan. The inside of a bank vault.

ACT I

(In the darkness, the sounds of many voices in chaos. Shouting, scream-
ing, and crying, along with -- slamming, banging, paper rustling --
all of these sounds flood the stage in a frenzied confusion.)

MAN #1. Down! Down!!
MAN #2. Get the fuck down!!
SABINA. Oh my God!
FELIZ. Please...
MAN #2. What did I say? What the fuck did I say?
FELIZ. Please don't hit him again!
MAN #2. No one talk!! No one says a goddamn thing!!
MAN #1. Hey...hey! Get away from that!
FELIZ. I'm sorry. I'm sorry I just...
MAN #1. Get over here now! All of you! You too, Shaft!
OAKLEY. Okay, okay...please...don't--
MAN #1. Kill you is what I'll do!! Now move!!

(Pause.)

SABINA. But that's the...
MAN #1. Just do it!

7

RYAN. Wait, what are you doing?

SABINA. Oh, God, please don't put us in there!

MAN #1. SHUT THE FUCK UP! EVERYONE GET IN THERE! NOW!!

MAN #2. Anyone says a word, and I'll come back here and fucking kill you.

(The sounds of intense struggle, people being pushed, more yelling, then the sound of a very large door being shut with some finality. Long silence. Lights up on the insides of a bank vault. A huge steel door at the center dominates the stage. Five people stand shocked, sweating and breathing heavily. For a long moment, no one speaks. Until-.)

FELIZ. Is everyone okay?

SABINA. Shhh.

(Everyone stares at the safe door waiting for something to happen. After another moment--)

FELIZ. Is anyone hurt? Did they hurt anyone?

SABINA. I'm fine.

RYAN. Me too.

FELIZ. Good. That's good.

SABINA. Shhhhhh!

(Again everyone stares at the door.)

RYAN. What are they doing?

FELIZ. Hopefully leaving.

RYAN. I can't believe this. I mean, I really can't believe this.

FELIZ. We're safe now. It's over.

RYAN. Right. That's right. We're in here and they're out there.

FELIZ. They got what they wanted. They'll be gone soon.

(RYAN looks around, panicked.)

RYAN. This is the safe?

SABINA. Be quiet. They said they'd come back here and shoot us.

FELIZ. That's not...the most important thing right now is to remain calm, collected, and in control. Everyone take a deep breath.

(The group takes a collective breath. For a moment it seems to work. Then, suddenly--)

RYAN. They said that? That they'd kill us? I didn't hear them say that.

SABINA. *(Snapping)* Oh, Christ! I can't take it. I just can't take it! I mean there was a gun in my face!

FELIZ. Sabina!

SABINA. He's waving it around, and I'm trying to do what he wants, but he keeps pointing it in my face.

FELIZ. It's okay. We're alive.

SABINA. *(Looking at the group.)* I mean. .a gun in anyone's face would make them nervous, right? Right?

(Truss and Oakley, each for different reasons, sit down. Blood streaks the side of OAKLEY'S head where he has been struck.)

FELIZ. Quiet. Yes...everyone's scared. It's a frightening thing.

SABINA. Right. Anyone would have freaked out.

FELIZ. *(Secretive)* Did you get to the...you know?

(Pause.)

SABINA. There was a gun in my face, Feliz.

FELIZ. *(To herself.)* No one's going to know now.

SABINA. I mean, it's not like this happens every day.

RYAN. No one's gonna know what?

FELIZ. Nothing. It's okay, it's fine.

SABINA. *(Realizing)* Oh, my God, could we be running out of air here?

FELIZ. Wait.

SABINA. Can we breathe in here?

RYAN. What?

SABINA. The air smells a little stale.

FELIZ. Let's not go there.

SABINA. Will air be a problem soon?

FELIZ. Everyone, please! The worst part is over. We're unharmed and out of danger. Let's try and stay positive.

OAKLEY. *(Dazed)* What happened?

SABINA. I think we're running out of air.

FELIZ. We're not running out of air.

SABINA. I think we should try not to breathe.

FELIZ. There is air in here, Sabina.

SABINA. How can you be so sure? Everything is...so...close.

FELIZ. We're fine.

SABINA. No, no. We're not fine. We need to conserve air.

RYAN. Hold on.

(SABINA points to FELIZ.)

SABINA. You're old. You'll be feeling it before any of us.

FELIZ. Excuse me?

SABINA. Seriously, you could drop any minute.

FELIZ. I'm fine.

SABINA. Now you're fine. But when the air goes...

RYAN. Excuse me, how much air do we have in here?

FELIZ. Stop worrying about the air. This will be over before we know it.

OAKLEY. What will?

RYAN. It will?

FELIZ. It will, dammit.

(The two have a moment -- calm and reassuring. Until...)

SABINA. Okay, nobody breathe.

FELIZ. Would you stop already?

SABINA. But I don't want to suffocate, Feliz! I'm too young to suffocate! I have cats!

RYAN. She's right! No one is going to suffocate!

FELIZ. Thank you. Now, there's enough air in here for all of us to breathe. In the meantime, these people, if they haven't left already, will get what they want and leave. Everything will be just fine.

SABINA. You don't think they're coming back here?

FELIZ. I don't even know if they're still here.

OAKLEY. *(Still dazed.)* Who?

SABINA. What do you mean? You think they left?

FELIZ. I don't know.

SABINA. Well, you're suggesting it. That has to be based on something. Doesn't it? Doesn't it?

FELIZ. Well, usually, criminals who rob banks don't just hang around and wait for the cops to show up. It's only logical that they've either left or are on their way.

(Silence. And then.)

TRUSS. If that's true, why are we in here then?

(Everyone stops and turns to TRUSS. In relation to everyone else he seems cool, collected, almost completely unconcerned. He speaks in an eerily detached way, as though he were going over a grocery list.)

FELIZ. Excuse me?

TRUSS. If those criminals just wanted to rob the bank and leave, why did they put us back here and leave all this money?

RYAN. I'm sorry...who are you?

SABINA. What are you saying?

TRUSS. I'm saying if this was just a "run and gun," like you say, they would have left us where we were and took the rest of this. *(TRUSS points to a pile of money half knocked out of wall safe.)* There were other rooms, other offices they could have put us in, too...but they didn't. They chose this safe.

RYAN. What are you getting at?

TRUSS. We're hostages.

RYAN. What?

SABINA. Oh, my God, really?

TRUSS. That's why we're in here, as opposed to somewhere else in the bank.

FELIZ. Wait a minute.

TRUSS. *(Calm but forceful.)* Something spooked them while they were robbing the bank and it made them put us in here.

OAKLEY. Holy shit! We're in the safe.

SABINA. Something? What, what something?

TRUSS. *(Nonplussed)* The police.

SABINA. And why would they put us in here?

FELIZ. Hold on, now.

TRUSS. Well, if we were out in front, any cop could see how many of us there were. Why bother with that kind of behavior unless the cops were already here?

SABINA. We're hostages.

FELIZ. You don't know that's true.

RYAN. Yah, they could have just as easily put us in here so no one walking down the street could see us. Give them more getaway time.

TRUSS. Maybe. But you have to admit that because we are in here, they can now tell the police anything they want and no one will be the wiser. We're their safety net.

FELIZ. That doesn't mean this is a hostage situation.

RYAN. She's right. We don't know for sure what the status is just yet.

TRUSS. We don't know otherwise.

SABINA. We're a safety net.

RYAN. No, look, if we just keep our composure and not cause any problems for anyone...we will be out of here.

TRUSS. In body bags.

FELIZ. We have to wait this out.

RYAN. I agree. Inaction is the best form of action in the absence of any information.

FELIZ. He's right.

SABINA. Is he?

TRUSS. If he's not, and things don't go well for those guys out there, they will kill us--

RYAN. *(Overlapping)* That is jumping to conclusions--

TRUSS. *(Overlapping)*--one by one...BANG.

SABINA. We're going to die!

TRUSS. Oh, you'll be fine, initially. Women are left for last. They elicit more sympathy from the cops.

SABINA. Sympathy?

TRUSS. Sure. No one wants to see someone's wife or mother raped and shot in the head. It's bad television.

SABINA. I don't want to die!

RYAN. *(To TRUSS.)* Jesus Christ, man!

TRUSS. What? It's the truth.

FELIZ. That's your truth.

TRUSS. My truth will save all of our lives. What will yours do?

FELIZ. And you're getting everyone worked up.

TRUSS. Not a bad place to be if you want to survive.

SABINA. I don't want to be raped!

TRUSS. I don't think you have to worry about that.

(SABINA recoils from TRUSS' remark, as though she has just been struck.)

RYAN. Okay, everyone just stop. We don't know we're hostages. No one is going to get raped, and we're not going to run out of air. Someone -- the police, a passerby -- will be here very soon. Let's try and enjoy ourselves.

OAKLEY. We've been robbed!

EVERYONE. YES!

OAKLEY. Damn. Anybody see anything?

(RYAN indicates FELIZ.)

RYAN. You. You work in the bank, too, right?

FELIZ. Yes. I'm the manager.

RYAN. Great. Well, while this was going on, you must have hit an alarm button, right? There must be a silent alarm button?

FELIZ. There is.

RYAN. O-kay. Then they'll be here. Like you said, all we have to do is sit tight--

FELIZ. I never hit it.

RYAN. What?

FELIZ. They had me down on the floor before I could get to it.

SABINA. *(Accusing)* You didn't hit the alarm?

FELIZ. Neither did you. They had you down on the floor just as fast.

TRUSS. *(To himself.)* Oh, they're good.

RYAN. So what does that mean?

FELIZ. It means, it's possible that, for the moment, no one knows the bank is being robbed.

(SABINA begins pacing.)

SABINA. I'm new here! It's not my fault. I told you that button was too damn small.

RYAN. What about the other alarms? Don't you guys have some kind of trip wire or fail safe device that just automatically goes off on its own when the bank is being robbed?

SABINA. I have long nails. I like to keep them that way and that tiny little button...you said cut them but I...

RYAN. You know, some kind of back up plan? This is the computer age.

SABINA. I take care of myself, get a manicure every now and then, so what? I wax too, is that a problem now?

RYAN. Isn't there some kind of sensor, a psychic... omniscient...microchip that just knows when a robbery is taking place?

(Everyone stares at RYAN as though he were the dumbest man on the planet. Even SABINA has stopped pacing.)

TRUSS. "Psychic, omniscient microchip?"

RYAN. I'm just trying to think.

TRUSS. Don't try too hard.

RYAN. Hey.

FELIZ. You don't understand. I gave them the all-clear code and they took my keys.

SABINA. You gave them the code?

FELIZ. I had no choice!

TRUSS. Nice.

RYAN. They left...I think we should assume they left.

TRUSS. You would.

SABINA. Why don't you think someone would want to rape me?

TRUSS. *(Shrugging)* Too much work.

SABINA. Who the hell do you think you are?

TRUSS. Who do you think I am?

SABINA. Wha-- huh?

(RYAN sees a small camera that overlooks a section of the safe.)

RYAN. What about the security cameras?

FELIZ. What about them?

RYAN. Well, the cameras are there for security...so...so...I don't know...someone, somewhere, must watch the cameras. Right?

FELIZ. It's not that simple.

(OAKLEY pushes himself to his feet, blood still streaks the side of his head where he has been struck. He walks over to RYAN, breaking all "personal space" rules.)

OAKLEY. They came in straight-up gangsta style.

FELIZ. Oakley, tell them about the cameras.

OAKLEY. Why?

FELIZ. Because that's your damn job!

OAKLEY. Okay, okay. Well...I'm just minding my own business, and out of the corner of my eye I see this flash, and I'm thinking... "Okay...something's going down." But I got hit, so I don't see too good now--

FELIZ, The cameras, Oakley. Tell them about the security cameras.

OAKLEY. Oh...well, the security cameras are connected to the guard booth, and you're right, the guard on duty is supposed to sound the alarm if anything happens, but---

(RYAN addresses the security camera.)

    RYAN. Hey! Help!
    TRUSS. *(Quiet but intense.)* Keep your voice down!

*(SABINA and RYAN begin waving at the camera and speaking in an
    exaggerated whisper.)*

    RYAN. Help! Help us!
    SABINA. Help us, please!
    OAKLEY. Uh...guys?
    RYAN. We're in here! We've been robbed.
    SABINA. There may not be much air left! And we have an elderly
woman here!!
    FELIZ. You're wasting your time.
    SABINA. Please hurry!
    RYAN. Hello! Can you see us?
    OAKLEY. Yes, I can see you.
    SABINA. Can you hear us?
    OAKLEY. Yes, I can see and hear you.
    SABINA. Hello?
    OAKLEY. Yes?
    RYAN. Hello!
    OAKLEY. Hello.
    RYAN. Why do you keep answering us?
    SABINA. Help!
    OAKLEY. Because that would be me. I'm the one who monitors the
security cameras.

(RYAN and SABINA stop.)

    SABINA. What?
    RYAN. Come again?
    OAKLEY. The other guard called in sick this morning, so I'm the
only guard on duty.
    SABINA. But you're here!

TRUSS. *(Clapping his hands.)* Oh, they are so good.

RYAN. Damn!

FELIZ. We tried to tell you. All the cameras are just in-house.

SABINA. So no one knows we're in here? Oh my God, we'll run out of air before anyone comes to get us. We'll all turn blue.

OAKLEY. They hit me in the head.

SABINA. We will all be a bunch of dead, blue people.

RYAN. No one is turning blue.

SABINA. *(To FELIZ.)* How are you doing?

FELIZ. What? I'm fine.

SABINA. Do you feel light-headed?

FELIZ. No.

OAKLEY. I feel a bit light-headed.

SABINA. Seeing any spots?

FELIZ. Sabina, if you don't stop--

SABINA. *(Cutting FELIZ off.)* Wait a minute. There's people outside!

TRUSS. Maybe they've come to shoot one of us. You know, set the tone for a hostage situation.

RYAN. You're not helping, sir.

TRUSS. Define "helpful."

SABINA. Shush, shush. No. That's not what I meant.

OAKLEY. *(Feeling unsteady.)* They hit me real hard on the head, I think.

SABINA. I meant that people outside on the street might have seen something and called the police.

RYAN. Yah, there you go, the streets are always packed. This is New York.

TRUSS. Packed with people who are only looking for cabs and subways. Next.

RYAN. Are you always this negative?

TRUSS. Nothing negative about being a realist.

FELIZ. Look, the bottom line here is this: the alarm wasn't tripped. I'm assuming they fired the all-clear code and locked the doors. We could be in for a wait, but no one's going to die.

SABINA. Well, it's Saturday. That means no one, including the alarm company, will know this bank was hit 'til Monday morning.

FELIZ. It's not going to come to that. My husband will expect me home. When he sees that I haven't gotten in, he'll make the call and tell them I work at this bank.

OAKLEY. No he won't.

FELIZ. Oakley, please. The cops will be here.

(This sets in and, for a moment, offers a modicum of comfort. Until...)

TRUSS. Unless...the cops are already here because these guys fucked up, ergo they're pinned down bullshitting with some second rate, alcoholic, wife-beating hostage negotiator, who would just as soon see us spilled out on the streets so he can go home, get a drink, and tee off on the Missus before Letterman.

SABINA. *(Hyperventilating)* Oh, shit!

TRUSS. That's right, darling.

RYAN. Would you please stop doing that?

FELIZ. Really.

TRUSS. Why? Don't you get it?

RYAN. Get what?

TRUSS. Robbing a bank is a federal offense.

RYAN. So?

TRUSS. So, the ATF, not known for their sense of self-control, will show up. Which means snipers and a whole lead storm of heavy artillery.

OAKLEY. I think I'm swallowing my own blood.

RYAN. Your point?

TRUSS. Just that they'll have those two punks in there gabbing away, pretending to negotiate, all the while sneaking some crazy merc squad in through the vent shaft with the sole intention of putting a hole in the back of one of those grease ball's heads, hoping, only as an after-thought, that we don't get hit with friendly fire.

SABINA. Friendly fire.

RYAN. Friendly fire?

OAKLEY. Yup. I'm swallowing my own blood.

TRUSS. Collateral damage, a couple of us go down to secure their main directive.

SABINA. Main directive.

RYAN. Main directive?

TRUSS. Their money. They'll protect it at any cost. If we get shot up in the process they still get their money, go home, and collect a paycheck.

(OAKLEY appears as though he may collapse.)

OAKLEY. *(Spitting)* I'm starting to see funny shapes.

FELIZ. Oakley, are you okay?

RYAN. Somebody should help him.

FELIZ. Can you hear me?

OAKLEY. Yes...but your voices are all starting to sound like...squeaky toys.

RYAN. Sit him down somewhere.

SABINA. Where?

OAKLEY. Squeak.

FELIZ. *(Obviously)* How about that chair?

RYAN. Yah. That's good.

(SABINA and FELIZ start moving to OAKLEY. As she does, SABINA sneers at TRUSS.)

SABINA. And I am not "too much work." I'll have you know, some people find me very attractive.

TRUSS. Please. They'd have to count a thousand Pamela Andersons just to get their pants off.

SABINA. SCREW YOU!!

TRUSS. One Pam Anderson, two Pam Anderson...

OAKLEY. Squeak.

SABINA. Bastard!!

TRUSS. ..three Pam Anderson...

RYAN. We should work together here! Bickering is not solving anything! So let's just shut up and focus!

OAKLEY. *(Pointing to his head.)* Yup...it's all squeaks and nonsense in here.

RYAN. Now, would you two find him a place to sit?

TRUSS. Why don't *you* find him a place to sit?

(Tense pause.)

RYAN. Excuse me?

TRUSS. I said, why don't you find him a place to sit.

RYAN. What are you talking about? The man is bleeding out of his ears. He needs help.

OAKLEY. I just need some soup and I'll be straight.

TRUSS. Oh, I'm not denying the man needs medical attention. He's obviously hemorrhaging from the brain. What I'm referring to is the assumption, by you, that you're in charge.

RYAN. I don't think I'm in charge.

TRUSS. Sure, you do.

RYAN. No. I just said we should find him a place to sit down.

OAKLEY. It's a motherfuckin' world.

TRUSS. Well, like I said, the content of your statement is fine. I just didn't vote for you to be the one who says it.

RYAN. Vote?? What is this...Survivor? This isn't a game, you crazy fuck! *(TRUSS immediately bristles with a tension that screams "violence" RYAN realizes he has gone too far.)* Okay, look. I'm sorry I said that...I didn't mean...

(RYAN walks to TRUSS but TRUSS'S sudden intensity stops him in his tracks without even laying a hand on him. If looks could kill, RYAN would be unconscious.)

TRUSS. Don't call me "crazy." Don't you *ever* call me "crazy" again.

RYAN. Sorry. I'm sorry.

FELIZ. Gentlemen, please.

(SABINA approaches RYAN and TRUSS.)

SABINA. We're gonna need something to stop his bleeding. What should we do?

TRUSS. Who are you asking?

SABINA. What?

TRUSS. Are you asking me, or are you asking him?

SABINA. *(Trying to answer the question.)* Am I missing something? He's bleeding?

RYAN. Oh, for Christ's sake! Look what you're starting. Will you stop?

TRUSS. No! I wanna know.

SABINA. I'm confused.

TRUSS. I think we need a leader, and I don't remember taking a vote. Do you?

SABINA. Oh...I see, ignore Sabina. Why am I never included in things like this? I'm here. I count! What the hell are we voting on?

FELIZ. Who has the bigger penis.

SABINA. You're voting on who has a bigger penis?

OAKLEY. *(More to himself than anyone in particular.)* Hot nuts...

RYAN. Fine, I don't care! You be the leader!

TRUSS. No.

RYAN. What?

TRUSS. No. Who said you could decide who the leader is? There you go again, making decisions for everyone.

SABINA. *(Nodding)* Oh. I get it.

RYAN. Okay. *(Referring to SABINA.)* What's your name?

SABINA. Sabina.

RYAN. Great. *(Referring to FELIZ.)* What's yours?

FELIZ. Feliz.

RYAN. Fine. *(Referring to OAKLEY.)* And you?

OAKLEY. Ahrrr...

(OAKLEY sits down on his own and begins staring off into space.)

FELIZ. His name is Oakley.

OAKLEY. O...ka...ly. Ok-ly.

RYAN. Right, Oakley. Well, he may have to waive his vote. Okay. So who votes for...

TRUSS. Truss.

RYAN. Russ?

TRUSS. Truss.

RYAN. Truss? Okay...who votes for Truss to be the leader?

(Pause. Everyone looks to one another, confused.)

TRUSS. You're confusing them.

RYAN. How can I be confusing them?

TRUSS. They don't know who to vote for because they can't make an educated decision yet.

RYAN. They're not stupid.

TRUSS. Look. *(Indicating RYAN.)* Who wants...

RYAN. Ryan.

TRUSS. Who wants...*(With a gay flair.)*...Ryan to be the leader?

(Everyone holds the same look they had before.)

TRUSS. See?

(TRUSS addresses the group once more.)

TRUSS. Who wants to be a rainbow?

RYAN. *(Throwing his hands up in the air.)* This is insane. I give up. I nominate Truss! And since I'm the only one who voted, you win unanimously. Congratulations. Your parents will be very proud.

TRUSS. *(Menacing)* What did you just say about my mother?

(FELIZ perks up like a light has just gone off in her head.)

FELIZ. My cell phone! I completely forgot! I have a cell phone!

(FELIZ retrieves her cell phone from her pocket.)

RYAN. *(Retrieving his cell phone.)* Oh shit!

(FELIZ and RYAN begin dialing, frantically. SABINA looks on. TRUSS watches, sullenly.)

FELIZ. Dammit! I'm not getting a signal.

RYAN. Hello?

FELIZ. Nothing! Not even *one* bar!

RYAN. Hello?

SABINA. What kind of phone do you have?

FELIZ. Nokia.

SABINA. I have Nokia. The new, little one. I got it because it looks cute and it comes in tons of colors.

RYAN. Hello?

SABINA. Mine's red. Perfect, right? It's like the emergency phone in the White House on West Wing. Do you have reception problems in Manhattan?

FELIZ. Not really.

SABINA. What service do you have?

FELIZ. You mean, how many minutes?

SABINA. Yeah, that too, but what's the company? AT&T? Sprint? Verizon?

FELIZ. AT&T.

SABINA. Oh...I heard AT&T service sucks in Manhattan. But if you're in...like, LA...or somewhere other than this city, it's great. The problem is, I'm in this city all the time, so I'm with Sprint. I'm thinking of moving to LA, but I like New York. I love New York. I think it's all the buildings, you know?

FELIZ. Yeah, the buildings are beautiful, very old. You don't find that in LA.

SABINA. What?

FELIZ. I agree. I'm agreeing with you. I love New York for its buildings, too.

SABINA. No. It's the buildings' fault you don't get good service in Manhattan.

FELIZ. Oh...I thought...

SABINA. Yeah, the signal bounces around from building to building like a pinball. It makes it harder for the thing to find it's satellite or something.

(RYAN is pacing back and forth on his cell phone. He finally gets through to someone.)

RYAN. Hello? Yes! Is this 911? Hello, can you hear me? Yes...911? I'd like to report a robbery.

(All eyes focus on RYAN.)

FELIZ. You got through?

SABINA. Tell them about my cats.

FELIZ. *(To SABINA.)* Shush!

RYAN. *(Waving them to be quiet.)* A ROBBERY! Can you still...hello...yes I can hear you, can you hear me? *(RYAN moves to another spot in the vault.)* Can you hear me? Yes!

SABINA. My cats will worry.

FELIZ. Would you just stop?

RYAN. Yes. Yes! Hello! Hello, I'm locked in a safe. I mean, we're locked in a safe, there are other people in here with me. Yes. Bandits...they locked us in the safe. At least two. Hello? Are you still there? Can you hear me? Yes, I can hear you. I'm here...I said, I can hear you. I know I'm breaking up, I said...hold on...hold on. *(RYAN is doing all he can to maintain that one bar of service: twisting, turning, cocking his head, moving sporadically through the space, then freezing.)* How about now? Can you hear me now? Hello? Hello? Do you hear me?

SABINA. The white, fluffy one is Debbie, and the smaller, mangy one is Scoops!

TRUSS. *(Shaking his head.)* One Pam Anderson, two Pam Anderson...

SABINA. Asshole!

FELIZ. You know, if you can't say anything nice or helpful, maybe you shouldn't say anything at all.

(RYAN vigorously waves at them to stop their bickering. The signal begins to fade as he tries one last effort to explain their situation.)

RYAN. WE ARE LOCKED IN A SAFE IN A BANK THAT'S BEING ROBBED. IT'S ON MOORE STREET, BETWEEN WATER AND PEARL. BY NEW YORK PLAZA. SEND HELP! Hello? Hello?

(RYAN'S heart is pounding. He is sweating and out of breath as he sits himself down on the floor, exhausted and defeated.) Dammit.

SABINA. Do you think they heard you?

RYAN. I don't know.

SABINA. But it's possible, right? They could have heard you.

RYAN. I don't know. I think it cut out before the last part.

SABINA. But you were talking to someone for awhile there. They might have heard the last part. Right?

RYAN. I guess.

(Long pause.)

TRUSS. "Bandits?"

RYAN. Huh?

TRUSS. Is this suddenly the wild west?

(TRUSS shakes his head sadly.)

RYAN. Bandits, yes. Robbers, thieves, whatever.

TRUSS. You sounded like a whacked-out crackhead just escaped from Bellevue.

RYAN. I sounded scared and frightened.

TRUSS. Fucked-up and confused, from where I'm standing.

RYAN. Look, I got through...okay? There's a chance, be it a small one, that the person on the other end heard me and is sending the cops as we speak.

FELIZ. That's right. It's possible.

TRUSS. No one's gonna send a frickin' metermaid, let alone the cops, based on that phone call! Besides, the cops are already here!

RYAN. I did my best!

TRUSS. Your best blows!

RYAN. Well, at least I tried! I don't see you jumping in to do anything. You're the leader now. Why don't you stop complaining and lead!

FELIZ. Gentlemen...

RYAN. Look at you. You don't even have a cell phone.

TRUSS. Just because I'm not going to rot my brain with those nasty cancer rods doesn't mean I'm not a good leader. I don't buy into popular culture, so what? Big deal. I'm not some compulsive cell phone talker. That's everyone's problem to begin with. Too much talking. We are a culture of "talkers." Not a "doer" in sight. That's your problem straight off, pal.

RYAN. What the hell does that mean?

TRUSS. I think you know exactly what that means.

RYAN. Oh, whatever, you crazy freak!

(TRUSS, in a fit of rage, grabs the cell phone out of RYAN'S hand, throws it down on the floor, and begins stomping on it.)

TRUSS. How do you like that? Huh? You like that? You're the freak, you're the freak! You want a leader? You want someone to lead? There! There's my first executive decision!

(Pause)

RYAN. Jesus...

SABINA. That was a nice phone.

FELIZ. You ruined the only phone that worked.

TRUSS. No one heard him and if they did, it doesn't matter! The cops are already outside negotiating with these two...bandits. *(TRUSS looks over at RYAN for effect.)* The only way out of here is from the inside. Otherwise, we wait it out and hope this ends before one of us gets shot in the head or flops over from dehydration.

SABINA. That's right. He's right about that. We do need water! And food! There's no food, either. What are we going to do about food?

TRUSS. We could always eat your ass.

SABINA. Fuck you!

TRUSS. Just one of those cheeks could feed us for a week.

RYAN. You just destroyed our best chance.

TRUSS. Our best chance of getting out of here has nothing to do with a cell phone.

RYAN. Then you know something we don't.

TRUSS. Oh, I know that much is true.

RYAN. Care to enlighten us?

FELIZ. Yes...go ahead...we're listening.

TRUSS. Well. Bank manager over here seems to think they're gone;

got the codes and the keys. Way to protect my money, by the way. Now I think these guys are no bullshit. They have a perfect plan. But they slipped up, otherwise we wouldn't be in here staring at their haul. We've been taken hostage, people, and we have to plan for that.

RYAN. How the hell do we plan for being hostages?

TRUSS. By refusing to be one.

RYAN. What?

SABINA. I don't understand.

TRUSS. If 9/11 taught us anything--

FELIZ. Oh, for God's sake...

TRUSS.--it's that you take things into your own hands, or else--

FELIZ. Those aren't terrorists out there.

TRUSS. Does it matter? Whether they have a political agenda or are just looking for beer money? Let me answer that for you: no...it doesn't. Dead is dead. And that's exactly what I'm not going to be when all of this is said and done. At the end of the day, long after this becomes "Breaking News" I plan to be home watching every last dirty movie on Skin-a-max.

SABINA. Pig.

TRUSS. Thank you.

RYAN. You're not making any sense.

FELIZ. Just what is it that you think we should do?

TRUSS. Right now, we're hostages. We're victims. To be blunt, we're as good as dead already. When they come through that door to make an example of us to the police, we have to show them something different.

SABINA. How?

TRUSS. By taking them out.

(Silence. Then, finally, everyone speaks at once.)

RYAN. *(Same time.)* That is the dumbest...

FELIZ. *(Same time.)* I don't know...

TRUSS. *(Same time.)* What's to know?

RYAN. *(Same time.)*...most reckless...

FELIZ. *(Same time.)* How could we...

TRUSS. *(Same time.)* I'll tell you all exactly what to do...

RYAN. *(Same time.)*...arrogant, delusional...

TRUSS. *(Same time.)* If you want to live, you'll listen to me.

RYAN. *(Same time.)*...egomaniacal...

SABINA. Maybe he's right!

(Everyone stops and looks at SABINA.)

RYAN. *(To SABINA.)* You can't possibly be serious.

SABINA. I know, I know. He's a slug.

TRUSS. You'd know.

SABINA. I would. But...they looked like killers.

RYAN. That doesn't mean--

SABINA. What...that they are? Do you want to take that chance? I don't.

RYAN. We can't just assume the worst.

TRUSS. I suppose you'd rather we all just talk.

(TRUSS cocks his head.)

RYAN. Look--

TRUSS. Shhh. Did you hear that?

SABINA. What?

TRUSS. I heard them.

SABINA. You did?

RYAN. I didn't hear anything.

TRUSS. Were you listening?

RYAN. Oh, come on, now...

TRUSS. Shhh. They're just outside.

RYAN. No.

FELIZ. I agree.

SABINA. Are you sure?

(Tense pause as everyone, on edge, waits to hear the sound that TRUSS is talking about, until--)

OAKLEY. You guys cold? *(Everyone turns to find OAKLEY sitting down and looking like hell. Blood has dried to the sides of his face, and his skin is a chalk-white.)* Has anyone come for us? Is there a doctor?

SABINA. We have to do something for him.

TRUSS. Like what? Do you see any doctors around? He's bleeding internally. We couldn't stop it if we tried.

OAKLEY. Oh, fuck. *(OAKLEY pushes himself to a standing position, wobbling around for balance.)* My head. I can't feel the side of my head.

FELIZ. Just keep pressure on it.

OAKLEY. You guys gotta help me. Did you call a doctor? I need help.

FELIZ. It's not that easy, Oakley.

OAKLEY. Help me!! Somebody, help me, please!

TRUSS. If he keeps shouting, he's going to agitate them into making a mistake.

(Everyone stares, not knowing how to help.)

OAKLEY. Help me! Somebody, help me, please!
FELIZ. Oakley. It's gonna be okay.
OAKLEY. Feliz, I need help.
FELIZ. We're doing everything we can, but...
OAKLEY. I smell almonds!
TRUSS. Shut him up.

(OAKLEY grabs onto nearby SABINA for balance, hoping for her help but pulling her around like a doll, bleeding all over her.)

SABINA. Don't do that.

OAKLEY. Help me, lady. Will you help me, please?

SABINA. Please...you're...someone get him off me. He's bleeding all over me! Jesus!!

OAKLEY. Ahhhh!! My head!! My fucking head!!

(OAKLEY is out of control, spitting and moaning.)

FELIZ. Oakley, please...

OAKLEY. I'm in the safe!

SABINA. He's gonna die on me!!

TRUSS. We're all gonna die if he doesn't shut up.

OAKLEY. I'm in the safe, come and get me!

SABINA. Get him off, he's hurting me!

FELIZ. Help her!

TRUSS. I'll shut him up if he doesn't calm down.

RYAN. What am I supposed to do?

(A bewildered RYAN looks around the room and comes up with nothing. He then slips a black boot off his foot and awkwardly rushes OAKLEY with the fat rubber heel. BIP! RYAN taps OAKLEY in the back of the head with it. OAKLEY spins around, more annoyed than hurt by the blow, and in the process puts SABINA in between them.)

OAKLEY. What are you...? Oh, bring it on!

(RYAN backs up, flustered. SABINA is now caught in the middle of the fight.)

SABINA. Oh, Jesus. Whoa!

(TRUSS, who's been watching with disgust, grabs the boot from RYAN'S hand and this time swings hard across OAKLEY'S left temple. BAM! OAKLEY goes down hard, letting go of SABINA in the process. TRUSS shakes his head as he looks at the boot in his hand, then drops it. Long pause.)

TRUSS. Pretty nimble there, slick.

(At once FELIZ kneels at OAKLEY'S fallen body. RYAN paces, slightly embarrassed. TRUSS moves to the safe door and cocks his head listening for any movement outside.)

RYAN. I'm sorry. I...is he okay? *(FELIZ is down checking for a pulse, her ear by his mouth.)* Is he...oh man...is he? I didn't know what to...he was freaking out, she was screaming...and...is he...

FELIZ. He's breathing but he's in real bad shape.

(SABINA pushes FELIZ and RYAN aside to get to OAKLEY, unaware of his condition.)

SABINA. Listen, you dirty little motherfucker! If you ever lay a hand on me again, I will bust your nut so far up your ass...*(She kicks at him, connecting once. RYAN and FELIZ restrain SABINA, pulling her back.)* I'm not taking that, no! I do not accept that kind of behavior. No! It's bullshit...he can't just...is he dead? Oh, my God! Oh, my God! Sir, are you dead?

FELIZ. He's not dead. Sit her down please and clean her up.

SABINA. I'm sorry, I didn't mean to hurt him.

RYAN. *(Taking SABINA to sit.)* You didn't.

SABINA. *(Turning on RYAN.)* You! What were you thinking? Your shoe?

RYAN. I was trying to help.

SABINA. With a shoe? You just pissed him off more.

RYAN. It's all I could come up with.

SABINA. Really? What about the chair? You could have punched him? I mean...shit.

RYAN. I don't know...I...

SABINA. That was dicey. And I didn't know if you were coming after me or coming after him!

RYAN. Just drop it.

SABINA. Fine.

RYAN. I'm sorry.

(SABINA sizes him up with a glance.)

SABINA. Hmmm.

(TRUSS listens at the door.)

TRUSS. I don't hear them anymore. What happens when he wakes up?

FELIZ. I don't know if he's going to wake up, young man. If we don't get him some medical attention soon he might...

(FELIZ trails off.)

TRUSS. It's that kind of thing that's gonna get us all killed.

FELIZ. That's your opinion, and to be perfectly honest, your opinion recklessly endangers us.

TRUSS. Well, if my opinion is wrong, nothing happens. If yours is, all of us are dead. Whose opinion is recklessly endangering everyone now? *(FELIZ cannot debate this point.)* I'll tell you all this, if he wakes up and gets a case of Tourette's like that again, we're gonna have to do something.

RYAN. Like what?

TRUSS. Well, I'm not going to tap him with my boot, if that's what you mean.

RYAN. *(Nervous)* Hey look, there's no need...

TRUSS. He's holding us back. Now I don't know about you, but I'm not okay with that.

RYAN. What are you saying we should do? Tie him up and gag him?

TRUSS. You know what dingos do when one of the pack is injured?

(Pause)

FELIZ. No.

TRUSS. Eat them.

RYAN. Jesus!

SABINA. I'm not eating anyone!

TRUSS. I'm not saying we should eat the man. I'm merely offering up an analogy. Like it or not, we are now a pack. The pack stays together. If that means sacrificing one so the pack goes on-

RYAN. We're not a pack of dingos! We're not a herd, or a gaggle, or a school, or anything else except stuck here.

TRUSS. And how long do you imagine we'll be stuck here for?

RYAN. When we measure the total of our lives, the time spent in

this safe will seem like a flash of light.

(Slight pause; everyone is a little stunned by RYAN'S statement.)

TRUSS. Are you high?
SABINA. You lost me, too.
RYAN. I'm just saying...
TRUSS. What? That we sit and wait 'til Oakland wakes up, goes into his *Apocalypse Now* routine and gets us shot. You know who you're like? You're like that...
FELIZ. His name is Oakley.
TRUSS. What?
FELIZ. His name is Oakley, not Oakland.
TRUSS. Oakley, right. That's what I said.
FELIZ. No. You said Oakland.
TRUSS. What? Okay, fine, Oakley. His name is Oakley. *(TRUSS turns back to RYAN.)* Now *you*. You're like that...religious guy in the Bible...what's his name?
RYAN. I don't know.
TRUSS. *(Getting frustrated.)* He waited and waited but...shit. *(TRUSS turns to FELIZ.)* I lost my train of thought now. You confused me with that Oakley thing.
FELIZ. I'm sorry, I didn't mean to confuse you.
TRUSS. Ahhh...forget it. It's fine. His name is Oakley. I knew that. I knew his name. It's not what I was talking about.
FELIZ. Something about wild dogs.

(TRUSS regains his focus.)

TRUSS. Dingos. The point is, Oakley is a liability. Did you see those guys out there? We're not talking about some unemployed stump whose plan is to hand the teller a note and hope she doesn't see the gun in his coat pocket is really a pencil. This type of job takes planning, it takes skill, and it takes balls. Armed robbery on a bank is an automatic twenty-five in the pen. You think a little homicide is gonna get in their way? *(Pause)* You may not value your own lives, but I value mine. The truth is, I don't care how unpopular I am in this safe right now. It makes no difference to me how uncomfortable you are with violently taking power out of their hands before they ultimately hurt us. This is not about giving some criminals the "benefit of the doubt." This is about survival, and I will not sit idly by if he sounds off again. *(TRUSS walks over and picks up RYAN'S boot. He casually hands it to him.)* Here. I reloaded it for you.

(TRUSS shakes his head and walks away.)

SABINA. *(Waiting until TRUSS is out of earshot.)* You think he's an Aries?

RYAN. I think he's an asshole.

SABINA. But is he right?

RYAN. I...I can't be sure just yet.

SABINA. When will you be sure? After I'm dragged off, sodomized, and then shot?

RYAN. What? No.

SABINA. It's so easy for you to be cavalier, you're a guy! I'm a victim; men like the ones outside can smell it a mile away. Hell, I even victimize myself!

RYAN. Umm...

SABINA. *(Pointing to FELIZ.)* Who do you think they're gonna violate? It sure as hell won't be her. So shut up!

RYAN. I didn't say anything.

FELIZ. We need to stop the bleeding.

TRUSS. *(From upstage.)* Use your socks.

(RYAN looks to TRUSS, then to SABINA. In a huff he takes off his socks and hands them to FELIZ.)

FELIZ. He needs to be looked at as soon as possible.

RYAN. How long before it gets serious?

FELIZ. I don't know. I don't know what I'm doing. He needs a doctor, I know that much. *(RYAN runs his fingers through his hair, frustration building.)* Listen, my husband is going to start wondering where I am in a few hours. He's a smart man, he'll call the police. I think Oakley will hold out until then. Any longer and...

SABINA. So no matter what's happening out there, you're saying someone will call the cops?

FELIZ. Eventually, yes.

SABINA. And they'll come and get us out?

FELIZ. Yes.

RYAN. *(Checking his watch.)* So that gives us, like, three hours. Give or take.

SABINA. But what if they're already out there?

(Slight pause.)

FELIZ. Let's try and make him as comfortable as we can until then.

RYAN. How?

SABINA. Take off his pants? *(Everyone cocks their heads.)* What? It helps me get comfortable.

RYAN. Let's move him over there. *(RYAN tries to lift OAKLEY as FELIZ and SABINA start clearing an area up-stage. RYAN, pauses, realizing he can't do it alone.)* Yo, Truss? A little help?

(TRUSS marches down stage.)

TRUSS. Funny, you strike me as someone who works out.

RYAN. Would you just help me?

TRUSS. Go do some push-ups. I got this.

(RYAN thinks better of engaging him and, quite honestly, doesn't like being around TRUSS.)

RYAN. He's all yours.

(TRUSS bends over to scoop OAKLEY'S legs up, when he feels something protruding from his ankle. He lifts OAKLEY'S pant leg and finds a chrome .22 revolver in a holster. He quickly covers the gun back up, looks around making sure no one saw, then casually slips the pistol out of its holster and into his waistband.)

TRUSS. *(Dragging OAKLEY to his resting place.)* Why do you continually assume we're alone?

RYAN. Because it's the most logical conclusion.

TRUSS. If I told you this morning you'd be robbed and locked in a safe, would you think that was logical?

RYAN. Why do you always go after me, man?

TRUSS. *(He thinks for a beat.)* Because you're the most logical one to go after.

(TRUSS chuckles to himself.)

RYAN. Funny. Very funny. *(RYAN steps to the side and motions Truss to follow. TRUSS warily moves over to RYAN.)* What's the deal, brother? I mean, I'm trying to get through this just the same as you.

TRUSS. Well...I don't think that's particularly true...dude.

RYAN. How so?

TRUSS. I know you. I know your type.

RYAN. What type is that?

TRUSS. *(Leaning in close.)* All front, no backbone.

RYAN. If you got something to say, say it.

TRUSS. All the answers are easy for you because it involves you doing nothing. I bet you do nothing all day. That's what's unmistakably wrong with the world. You...and your apathy.

RYAN. *(He stares, unable to respond, then.)* Whatever.

TRUSS *(Mocking)* Yah. Whatever. *(RYAN gives up and moves to the spot FELIZ and SABINA have cleared.)* Our only chance of getting out of here is to act as a group, a pack.

SABINA. Like dingos.

TRUSS. We have to plan a course of action, which means we have to agree on some fundamental things. One: can we all agree this bank was robbed today?

(Everyone looks at each other, nods their heads slowly, and answers.)

GROUP. Yes.

TRUSS. Two: whoever these men were, they had guns and very bad intentions?

(Again the group slowly nods.)

GROUP. Yes.

TRUSS. *(Pointing to OAKLEY.)* Three: the same men who did that to him, these felons, these thugs who beat his head in for nothing more than earning a living, locked us in this safe?

GROUP. Yes.

TRUSS. So, just by answering those three simple questions, can we all conclude that there is at least the possibility that we are still in grave danger? Is there anyone in this safe that would risk another's life thinking otherwise? *(The group falls silent.)* There is no time for dissension, and no room for mistakes. What we do from here on out dictates our future; it's that simple. It doesn't have to be popular. It has to be effective.

(Long pause. The group appears swayed by TRUSS. Finally...)

SABINA. So...what do we do?

TRUSS. For starters, we need to know as much about them as we can.

SABINA. Like what?

RYAN. There were two of them, we know that.

TRUSS. Two in the bank. If they're as good as I think, they have a driver spotting outside. That's three. What else do we know?

RYAN. One had a .357. Magnum and the other had a sawed off Remington 12 gauge. *(All look to RYAN. Feeling everyone's stare.)* My father had a lot of guns. He collected them.

TRUSS. Well, well, well. Didn't we just get a little less boring. Do you know how to shoot?

RYAN. I'm not gonna shoot anybody, but yah...I know how to fire a weapon.

TRUSS. Good. Bank manager, do you know what they took?

FELIZ. I'm not sure what they got.

SABINA. They emptied my box and a few others. It couldn't have been much.

FELIZ. That's probably why they went for the safe. *(FELIZ motions to the mess in the vault.)* As you can see, it's going to be a while before we figure out what they took from in here. What does it matter what they took?

TRUSS. We need to know the enemy to fight the enemy. Why risk hitting the safe?

FELIZ. Saturdays are big volume days.

TRUSS. So? That means you guys are loaded.

FELIZ. No. Saturdays are mostly withdrawals.

SABINA. Nasdaqers want their money for the weekend.

FELIZ. The most they could have gotten from the cash boxes is maybe ten, fifteen thousand.

TRUSS. How much is in this safe?

FELIZ. *(Going over to the log book.)* Well...187,000 dollars to be exact.

TRUSS. Bingo!

(The sound of light tapping from the walls. Everyone stops.)

RYAN. Shhh. Do you hear that?

SABINA. What is that now?

TRUSS. Wait. Wait. Wait!

FELIZ. It's coming from the walls.

TRUSS. Shit.

SABINA. What? What is it?

RYAN. Shhhh! *(The sound comes again.)* I definitely heard that.

TRUSS. It's started.

SABINA. What's started?

TRUSS. The police. They're trying to make contact.

SABINA. You think that's the police?

FELIZ. Through the wall?

TRUSS. I know, that's what worries me.

RYAN. It's not the police.

TRUSS. *(Sure)* It's the police.

RYAN. Maybe it's a hot water pipe.

TRUSS. They're panicking.

RYAN. It's plumbing.

TRUSS. No, no, no. Negotiations must be breaking down. They

weren't ready for this.

RYAN. Ready, for what? The heat to go on?

FELIZ. Ryan's right. I think you're overreacting.

TRUSS. Really? I think we're screwed.

SABINA. Why? Why would you say that?

TRUSS. They're surrounded -- cops, guns everywhere. Snipers in their positions. It's a frightening thing to see if you're not used to it. That much hardware pointing at you. They froze! And the cops take their silence as a sign to make a move.

SABINA. What does that mean, "move?"

TRUSS. They need to know where we are, so they're tapping around...for us.

RYAN. *(Moving to the wall.)* This is stupid. I'll prove to you, it's not the cops. I'm gonna tap back...

TRUSS. *(As if he's been scalded.)* No!

(RYAN jumps, momentarily showing his true fear.)

RYAN. What?

TRUSS. Back away from the walls.

FELIZ. Why?

SABINA. Are they coming for us or them?

TRUSS. *(Terrified)* Don't touch the walls! Everyone, get to the center of the room.

RYAN. Can we stop jumping to conclusions, here?

TRUSS. *(Emphatically to RYAN.)* Listen. It's time for you to stop being a problem and become part of the solution. Don't fuck this up for us. Now...GET AWAY FROM THE WALLS. Do it! *(The group, frightened, does as they're told.)* We have to be careful now. Their backs are against the wall out there. It's more dangerous than ever. If they come back here and find out we're communicating with the--*(More tapping. TRUSS freezes, genuinely afraid. He pulls himself together. Whispering)* We can't give those guys out there any reason to--

(OAKLEY sits up.)

OAKLEY. I ain't feeling...I think they hit me again. Those mother-fuckers. *(All eyes whip to OAKLEY, who looks like a ghost. More tapping from the walls.)* It was a club or something. Doctor's on his way, right? Why are you all standing in the middle of the...wait a minute. You hit me. I remember now. You!

TRUSS. This is bad.

(OAKLEY points to RYAN.)

OAKLEY. You little shit! Step away from him. I got this...

(OAKLEY reaches for his ankle holster, but finds nothing there.)

TRUSS. He's going to send them back here and they're going to find out about this tapping and panic.

OAKLEY. Son of a bitch! Give me my gun!

(OAKLEY stands and begins staggering about, trying to maintain focus.)

TRUSS. They will take their panic out on us!

OAKLEY. *(Yelling)* Where is my gun? Where is it?

RYAN. I...I'm sorry, I don't know what your talking about.

OAKLEY. Give me back my gun! He's got my gun, goddammit!

TRUSS. Both sides are under a lot of pressure out there. It's not going to take much. They'll snap.

FELIZ. Oakley, I think you should sit back down.

OAKLEY. He's got my gun! Right there, him!

TRUSS. They are going to torture and kill us!

FELIZ. Oakley, you're not in your right mind.

TRUSS. Noise.

FELIZ. *(To TRUSS.)* I know, I know. *(FELIZ turns back to OAKLEY.)* Just sit down and be calm. No one took your gun.

OAKLEY. I had it in my boot. Fuck y'all!

TRUSS. I can't allow this.

OAKLEY. Call me a doctor! And give me my gun!

TRUSS. What's it going to be, pack?

OAKLEY. Doctor! Now! Help! Why won't you help?!

(TRUSS puts his hands out, counting to five. Everyone just watches.)

FELIZ. *(To TRUSS.)* Wait.
OAKLEY. Help! Help me!
FELIZ. Oakley, please.

(TRUSS has finished his countdown. Still no response. OAKLEY runs to the safe door.)

OAKLEY. I'm in here! I'm in the safe! HELP!!

(Before OAKLEY can make it to the safe door, TRUSS attacks. He brings OAKLEY to the ground and looks to the group for some kind of response. He takes their silence as compliance and begins to strangle a very resistant OAKLEY. OAKLEY begins to fight -- legs kicking, gurgling, arms flailing -- it is a painful sound. FELIZ instinctively makes a move towards TRUSS in order to stop him, but is stopped herself by SABINA. The two share a look and then, along with RYAN, watch this all happen. TRUSS looks at them, not OAKLEY, as he continues to strangle him. Finally, OAKLEY stops struggling and slumps over -- dead. Only slightly winded, TRUSS disentangles himself from OAKLEY and stands up to face the others.)

FELIZ. Oh my God.

LIGHTS OUT. END OF ACT ONE

ACT II

(Time has passed. It's getting hot. OAKLEY'S body lies center stage. A struggle has taken place. RYAN is handcuffed to a metal post that comprises one of the bank's safety deposit boxes. TRUSS sits, appearing different, changed in some way. He's somber, withdrawn. SABINA lies sprawled out on the floor, her legs propped on the table which has been over turned. FELIZ sits dazed, clearly different as well. Something about her seems defeated.)

(After a long pause...)

RYAN. We're all going to hell. *(No one says a word.)* That man did not deserve that. He did not deserve to die. *(Pause.)* The sounds he made...that gurgling...twitching...*(Pause)* His eyes...the way they just bugged out and went cold...Jesus Christ, you just straight-up killed a man.

TRUSS. You want me to gag you, too?

FELIZ. *(Referring to RYAN'S handcuffs.)* Are those really necessary?

TRUSS. Yes.

RYAN. I told you, I had a panic attack. It won't happen again.

TRUSS. Right. I'm gonna set you loose so you can try and scratch my eyes out some more?

RYAN. Fuck you...lawn jockey. *(Pause. TRUSS does not respond. RYAN rattles his cuffs.)* Let me out of these. *(Another pause.)* I said let me the hell out of these so I can kick your ass!

43

TRUSS. If you trim your nails first, maybe I will...fag.

RYAN. Bastard!

SABINA. *(With a sudden surge of authority.)* Stop it! The two of you are driving me insane. (*SABINA discovers a canister of mace that presumably has fallen from OAKLEY'S belt during the struggle.)* Oh, mace. We could use this, right?

TRUSS. *(All business.)* Yes. *(Pause)* Why don't you hold onto it? For protection.

SABINA. Oh. Really?

TRUSS. Yeah.

SABINA. *(Awkward)* Ummm...thank you.

TRUSS. You're welcome.

(SABINA takes the mace and the two share an oddly sincere moment.)

RYAN. Hey! Hey! I hate to interrupt such a special moment, but he just killed that man! Does no one get that?

TRUSS. We.

RYAN. Excuse me?

TRUSS. Before you get all up on your high gay horse, let's not forget we all decided to do it.

RYAN. No.

TRUSS. We did.

RYAN. I didn't say anything.

TRUSS. And your silence spoke volumes.

RYAN. That's bullshit.

TRUSS. You're bullshit!

FELIZ. He's right. We all killed that poor man.

RYAN. Are you insane? I don't remember any of us wrapping our arms around Oakley and choking him to death.

FELIZ. We said nothing. We did nothing. We're just as culpable.

RYAN. Fine. If you want to feel that way, go right ahead. But I will not accept I killed anyone.

TRUSS. You're a coward!

RYAN. You're a murderer!

TRUSS. You sit there and judge me?

RYAN. Actually, you handcuffed me to a wall so I have to sit, but yes, I am judging you.

TRUSS. You criticize everyone but never do anything yourself.

RYAN. Like what? Choke out an innocent security guard? Would I be proactive then?

TRUSS. You think I enjoyed that?

RYAN. As a matter of fact, yes, I do.

(TRUSS converges on RYAN. There is a wildness in his eyes.)

TRUSS. I've never killed anyone in my life! I'm disgusted with what happened! *(TRUSS pauses for a moment to regain his composure. This is difficult for him.)* What I did was the right thing. What I did, I did for us. I did it for the pack.

RYAN. The pack? You can't possibly believe what you're saying.

TRUSS. If we let him go on like that, making all that noise, how long before they heard him screaming for his gun and came in here and bucked us down?

RYAN. No one came in, did they?

TRUSS. Because I did something. *(Pause)* That's right. So while you sit there with your damn nuts in your mouth deciding what's the best way to act, the clock ticks away and your options get fewer and far between. I made a decision and moved on it. I saved our lives.

RYAN. You ended a life.

TRUSS. I acted.

RYAN. You acted without thinking!

FELIZ. It doesn't matter. If we get out of here, we all leave murderers.

RYAN. Don't put me in the same category with that sadistic fuck.

FELIZ. I don't have to. You already are.

RYAN. Well I, for one, am not going to sit here and think--

SABINA. Oh, go cry to your gun-loving daddy!

RYAN. Whoa...what the hell?

SABINA. I've dated plenty of guys like you, you know? Always talking "morality," when what they really want is to get in your pants. Always bumming smokes and bail money, which you give them, only to find out, after they've dumped you and left you in debt, that daddy owns Macy's or some fucking pharmaceutical company.

RYAN. "Smokes and bail money?"

SABINA. You're a liar.

RYAN. About what?

SABINA. Everything!

RYAN. What have I lied about?

SABINA. Why were you in the bank today?

RYAN. Well, I...wait...what do you mean? Where are you going with this?

SABINA, How much was the check you deposited?

RYAN. What?

SABINA. How much money did you deposit today?!

RYAN. I...I don't remember.

SABINA. I'll tell you exactly how much, because I handled your transaction. You deposited a check for over ten thousand dollars.

RYAN. You're keeping tabs on me?

SABINA. You hit on me. I always remember the cheese balls who hit on me.

RYAN. I did not.

SABINA. You stood at the front of the line and let, like, five people pass you up. Then, when my teller number flashed, you took your turn.

RYAN. This is madness!

SABINA. Why would you do that then?

RYAN. I was filling out...the thing.

SABINA. Sure you were.

RYAN. The deposit slip.

SABINA. It took you a looong time to fill it out.

RYAN. Well, there's a lot of crap you need to put down on that little piece of paper.

SABINA. Yet you don't remember how much you deposited?

RYAN. What is this, the Spanish Inquisition?

SABINA. You can't even tell the truth about how much the check was.

RYAN. I told you, I don't remember!

SABINA. Don't remember hitting on me? Or don't remember why

you were in the bank in the first place? Which one is it?

RYAN. I...I'm not sure.

SABINA. I think you're a liar. I'm just getting it all out on the table.

TRUSS. *(Nodding)* Trust fund baby.

RYAN. No. I made my own way.

SABINA. Wouldn't be hard with daddy's company checks coming in every month.

RYAN. Where I get my checks has nothing to do with--

SABINA. You actually sit there, looking at us like your shit doesn't stink. You have blood on your hands too, daddy's boy, so stop bitching and catch up. *(OAKLEY'S body jerks.)* Ahhh! He moved. Oh, Christ.

TRUSS. Relax.

SABINA. Is that normal?

TRUSS. *(Nodding)* It's just residual air escaping from his stomach.

(OAKLEY'S body jerks again.)

SABINA. Okay, that's freaking me out.

FELIZ. Could we please cover him up and leave him in peace?

TRUSS. I need to get his belt and shoelaces first.

FELIZ. May I ask why?

TRUSS. We might be able to use all this stuff. You never know.

SABINA. Yeah, you never know.

TRUSS. *(Looks to SABINA.)* Come here. One, two, three. *(TRUSS pulls off OAKLEY'S belt as SABINA gets his laces.)* Take off that jacket so we can cover him up.

SABINA. Why this jacket? Why don't you use yours?

TRUSS. Just give me the damn jacket.

RYAN. But it's mine.

TRUSS. I don't care whose it is.

RYAN. I'm just saying, it's not hers to give to you.

SABINA. Fine. Take it. I don't want it anyway. *(SABINA gives TRUSS the jacket she wears around her waist. TRUSS puts it over the body of OAKLEY as SABINA walks over to RYAN, clearly disgusted by him.)* You know, you are a little gay.

RYAN. What? It's the principle. It has nothing to do with the jacket.

I'm not a fashion...you know what? Forget it.

(Long pause. Finally, FELIZ speaks.)

FELIZ. He had three kids. Just found out he was a grandfather.

RYAN. What? Oh. Yeah.

FELIZ. He bought the most incredibly...ugly dress for that baby. He wanted her to wear it the first time she met him.

RYAN. Yeah.

FELIZ. I said, "Oakley, that's...beautiful!" He said, "Ain't it? She's gonna look like a fuckin' princess." That was Oakley.

RYAN. You knew him well?

FELIZ. As much as you can know someone who nods off and sleeps all day. I knew he was a good person. Not like me. Not like us.

(RYAN glances to see if TRUSS or SABINA is listening to him. Neither is.)

RYAN. Look...it doesn't need to be like this. You could help me...get free.

FELIZ. What would you do if you were?

(Pause. And then, with a clunk, the safe goes completely dark.)

SABINA. Ahhhhh!

TRUSS. Get down! Down on the floor!

SABINA. Here they come.

RYAN. What? What's going on?

FELIZ. Hold on.

RYAN. What the fuck is going on?

TRUSS. Hit them hard and hit them fast! *(With the same clunk with which the lights went out, emergency lights flick on and bathe the vault in an eerie glow. Everyone is in a battle-ready position. Whispering.)* Wait for it. Wait.

RYAN. What's this now?

FELIZ. Emergency lights.

SABINA. What does that mean?

TRUSS. Cops cut the power. Typical.

SABINA. Are they coming in?

TRUSS. If they do, use your mace. Aim for the head. Once you hit your target, make a break for the sides of the safe where it's dark.

SABINA. Okay.

TRUSS. *(Addressing the group.)* If they come, stay covered until I make a move, then get into the shadows. Remember, if shit goes down, darkness is your friend.

RYAN. Uncuff me. I'm helpless.

TRUSS. Why? You're helpless either way.

RYAN. Fuck! I'm wide open here.

TRUSS. *(Mocking)* I thought no one was out there? I thought they left?

RYAN. *(Pleading)* Come on, man!

FELIZ. Maybe you should let him go. It's wrong to leave him like that.

RYAN. That's right. Toss me the keys.

FELIZ. We can't leave him chained up. It's not right.

RYAN. Throw me the keys. Please.

(Long pause.)

TRUSS. No.

RYAN. No?!

TRUSS. You're more helpful right where you are.

RYAN. But I'm the first one they'll go for.

TRUSS. Exactly. And when they do, I sneak behind them and take my shot.

(Truss pulls OAKLEY'S pistol from his waistband. RYAN, seeing TRUSS'S gun, begins an awkward and panicked dance to shimmy to some kind of cover as fast as he can.)

RYAN. Whoa! Don't shoot! Help. Please don't.

TRUSS. Quiet! I'm not going to shoot you. You're the decoy.

RYAN. Decoy? But I don't want to be the decoy.

TRUSS. Stop being selfish.

RYAN. Selfish? Just because I don't want to be sacrificed doesn't mean I'm selfish. Someone let me go.

(RYAN desperately looks around the safe.)

TRUSS. *(Pointing the gun at RYAN.)* You're going to stay right there and you're going to shut up. Got it? I'm not playing with you.

RYAN. Don't. Don't point that at me. It could go off. Stop. Please don't do that.

FELIZ. Don't point that at him.

RYAN. Stop...stop it!

TRUSS. Scared, Ryan? Good.

(TRUSS backs down and repositions himself. RYAN is beside himself with fear.)

RYAN. *(Panicking)* I can't be locked up like this. Please! Someone. Anyone! *(RYAN pulls at the cuffs, feeling the desperation begin to swell.)* Come on, come on, come on.

(FELIZ moves over to RYAN.)

FELIZ. It's going to be okay.

RYAN. Let me out. I have to get out of these. Now. *Now.*

SABINA. Did you hear that? I think I heard something!

RYAN. Ahh!

FELIZ. Shhh...it's okay. It's going to be okay.

RYAN. No, it's not.

(Everyone waits for something to happen. Nothing does. TRUSS refocuses on the unfolding event and begins to stealth towards the safe door, his gun out. RYAN reaches out to TRUSS as he passes and TRUSS, a little startled, points the gun at RYAN, who immediately cowers. As TRUSS continues to move towards the safe door,

SABINA now reaches out to TRUSS as he passes her, touching his pant leg and scaring the hell out of him. TRUSS recomposes himself and finally reaches the door. He listens intently.)

SABINA. Are they coming?

(TRUSS puts his hand to his lips indicating for SABINA to be quiet. He listens some more until, suddenly, his eyes widen and he zips back to his hiding place next to SABINA.)

RYAN. What? What??

TRUSS. I think I heard them moving out there.

SABINA. They're outside?

TRUSS. *(Checking the bullets in his gun.)* I'm not sure.

SABINA. What do you mean, you're "not sure?"

TRUSS. Just stay covered and get ready.

RYAN. Feliz, talk to me. Are they coming in? Did you see that!? What's happening with the lights?

FELIZ. It's after eight. The lights went off.

RYAN. Why?

FELIZ. I don't know, I've never been in the bank this late. Try to calm down. You're attracting more attention to yourself by squirming around.

RYAN. But you're the manager. Did the power get cut or do the lights automatically go off at eight?

FELIZ. I don't know, Ryan! I told you I've never been here this late, let alone in the safe. It's a question for Oakley.

RYAN. Right, and he's dead, so we can't ask him, can we? You're useless. You work at this place and you're useless.

FELIZ. I don't have all the answers, for Christ's sake! I'm trying my best to keep it together, not just for me but for everyone else, and I'm sick of it!

RYAN. He's not gunning for you, Feliz! He's not using you as bait! He's had it in for me from the start.

FELIZ. *(Snapping)* Goddamnit! I wish they would come in here and get it over with. I can't stand it anymore.

RYAN. That lunatic has a .22.

FELIZ. I don't know if I can do this anymore.

RYAN. You know whose gun that is, right?

FELIZ. Does it matter?

RYAN. Oakley's. That's Oakley's gun. Crooked son of a bitch had it all this time.

FELIZ. Ryan.

RYAN. He just let him go on accusing me. It was him all along!

FELIZ. I'm not a good person.

RYAN. He's gonna kill me, I just know it.

FELIZ. I just thought you should know.

RYAN. Know what?

FELIZ. You don't seem like the rest. I want you to know I'm sorry.

RYAN. "Sorry" doesn't help right now.

FELIZ. Well, I am. I'm sorry.

RYAN. Spare me your apology. Right now I need help. Wasn't your husband supposed to call, like, four hours ago?

FELIZ. I'm sure he did call.

RYAN. Well, where the fuck is he? How sure are you he'd call? Maybe he sketched out?

FELIZ. I work in a bank. We've discussed this situation before.

RYAN. Maybe this one time he went out or something.

FELIZ. No. I think maybe Truss is right. We're their hostages, otherwise someone would be here by now. *(Pause.)* Ryan? If I ask you a question, will you give me an honest answer?

RYAN. I don't know if this is the right time for twenty questions.

FELIZ. Why didn't you stop him from killing Oakley?

RYAN. Oh, come on.

FELIZ. Honestly.

RYAN. I don't know.

FELIZ. That's not honest.

RYAN. I froze. Okay? There.

FELIZ. I froze too, but why?

RYAN. What do you mean, "why?"

FELIZ. I know why I froze. I'm asking you.

RYAN. Your answer is just as good as mine.

FELIZ. Right. I don't know if I can live with that.

RYAN. That sicko right over there, that's who you should ask. (*The two stare at each other. RYAN looks over at TRUSS.*) You better hope I never get these off.

(Lights fade.

Lights up. Time has passed. The group is exhausted from the increasing heat and waiting for something to happen. TRUSS and SABINA are still behind cover. RYAN has not moved and FELIZ seems to be writing something in the safe's money log. The mood is somber but the immediate threat is gone.)

SABINA. I was wondering when you were gonna whip it out?

TRUSS. What?

SABINA. The gun. I saw you take it from Oakley.

(TRUSS rolls this around in his head.)

TRUSS. And you didn't say anything?

(SABINA smiles.)

SABINA. Are you hungry?

TRUSS. You got something?

SABINA. Maybe. *(SABINA looks around and pulls a candy bar from her boot. She handles it like drugs.)* Oh Henry.

TRUSS. What's in it?

SABINA. Chocolate, caramel, and peanuts.

TRUSS. What's the difference between an Oh Henry and a Snickers bar?

SABINA. I don't know. Nougat? Maybe.

TRUSS. Seems like they're all the same to me, just different packaging. It doesn't matter. I can't eat it. I'm allergic to nuts. Share it with the others.

SABINA. Really? But it's just chocolate, caramel, and peanuts.

TRUSS. Right. I'm allergic to nuts.

SABINA. You sure? I don't even know if it's real nuts.

TRUSS. You mean like fake nuts?

SABINA. Yeah.

TRUSS. I've never heard of fake nuts.

SABINA. You could pick them out.

TRUSS. I can't chance it. It's not the actual peanut I'm allergic to, it's the nut oil. If I so much as taste it, my throat swells up like a pillow and I can't breathe.

SABINA. That's horrible. I don't know what I would do. I couldn't eat a candy bar without nuts.

TRUSS. I'm sure you'd get by.

SABINA. That's a little underhanded, don't you think?

TRUSS. What?

SABINA. "I'm sure you'd get by?" What's that mean? I'd be thinner if I didn't eat chocolate?

TRUSS. Don't you fucking start. I can't eat nuts. That's it. Nothing more, nothing less.

(SABINA slowly lets it go.)

SABINA. I'm allergic to dust mites.

TRUSS. Oh, for fuck's sake! You're driving me insane. You know what? Go away. Just go over there.

SABINA. You're an asshole! I'm trying to share my Oh Henry with you and you somehow turn it into me being crazy. It's not my fault you can't eat the fucking thing. You know what? Fuck it. I try and try and where does that get me? Nowhere.

TRUSS. Beat it!

SABINA. No. You can't tell me what to do.

TRUSS. Fine. Stay then.

SABINA. Do you want me to stay?

TRUSS. Not really.

SABINA. Fine! I'm going to the bathroom. And guess what? I'm gonna pee in that corner over there and I don't care what you say.

TRUSS. Fine. I pissed over there myself.

SABINA. Fuck you!

TRUSS. Typical. You're such a girl.

SABINA. Oh, you are not gonna go there!

TRUSS. You are. You're such a girl. You have to piss every twenty minutes.

SABINA. Woman! And I have a small bladder.

(TRUSS considers this.)

TRUSS. Is that the reason? A weak bladder?

SABINA. Small bladder. Not weak.

TRUSS. You sure?

SABINA. Yes. Why? What the fuck is this?

TRUSS. You haven't been drinking water, have you?

SABINA. What? That's ridiculous. Where would I get water?

TRUSS. You tell me.

SABINA. There's nothing to tell.

TRUSS. Cuz it would be pretty disappointing to find you've been holding out on us all this time. First the candy bar, and now water?

SABINA. I tried to offer you the only food I have. I could have eaten it all by myself, but I was kind enough to share.

TRUSS. Don't you think bank manager might have wanted some? Or Ryan? Why just me?

SABINA. You asshole.

TRUSS. Everyone, listen up. Do you think I'm an asshole because she secretly offered me food and I refused?

SABINA. Don't.

TRUSS. I think I would be an asshole if I knew you had water and didn't tell everyone.

RYAN. She has water?

SABINA. No, I don't. Why are you doing this?

TRUSS. I thought you liked it all out on the table?

FELIZ. Hold on. What makes you think she has water?

SABINA. Yeah.

TRUSS. Every time I turn around, she's taking a piss.

SABINA. I have a small...

FELIZ. Is that true, Sabina?

SABINA. What?

FELIZ. Have you been drinking water?

SABINA. When?

RYAN. What do you mean, "when?" Don't let her dumb her way out of this.

SABINA. Excuse me? I don't think you have the right to talk. You're in lockdown.

FELIZ. Sabina, if you have water, you need to tell us.

TRUSS. Just tell us. Come on, we won't be upset if you tell the truth. I think everyone would love a swig of water, right?

GROUP. Yeah. Sure.

SABINA. I don't know what you're talking about.

TRUSS. Lying only makes it worse. If you come clean, we'll forget about it.

(SABINA thinks long and hard. Her hand nervously swings by her side under the group's heavy gaze. Finally...)

SABINA. It was in here already.

TRUSS. How?

FELIZ. How was it in here already?

SABINA. We only get one lunch break. One! I mean, in an eight-hour day, one meal is not enough. The human body doesn't function well when you're hungry. I've asked for more breaks, but you said, "No, that's not feasible." I asked if I could have a little something at my station; you said, "That's not professional." What was I supposed to do? Starve? Workers are more productive when they're fed! It's a fact. Okay? It's just my snacking place. I...I keep snacks in here for when I'm hungry. That's it. That's all.

TRUSS. Where?

SABINA. A little candy and something to drink. That's it.

TRUSS. Where is it?

(Pause.)

SABINA. The safety deposit boxes. Ones that no one uses. Don't get mad, Feliz.

TRUSS. Which one?

SABINA. That one. *(SABINA points to a safety deposit box on the wall.)* One nine seven five. It's out of the camera's view...and it's also the year I was born.

TRUSS. What's in there? Show us.

(SABINA walks to the box, looks around and opens the small door. She pulls out a half-pint of bottled water. SABINA has drunk most of it.)

SABINA. Here.

TRUSS. What else?

(SABINA pauses then reaches back to the box and pulls out a few gum-balls, and a small bag of Sour Patch Kids.)

SABINA. Just gum and some Sour Patch Kids.

(TRUSS walks over to SABINA, looks in the cubbyhole then sticks his hand in and pulls out an empty HoHo wrapper, holding it up for all to see.)

TRUSS. What's this?

SABINA. I ate that yesterday. I did. Smell my breath.

RYAN. Guilty. Lock her up.

TRUSS. This is the kind of shit I'm talking about. I'm so fucking disappointed right now.

RYAN. Lock her up, man.

SABINA. A fucking HoHo and some gum isn't going to kill anybody. They're snacks!

TRUSS. You'd be shot in some countries for this.

RYAN. He's right. Put her in these. We'll switch.

TRUSS. Bank Manager, pass this out. We all have to keep hydrated. Two caps every hour till it's gone except Sabina. She gets none.

SABINA. What!?

RYAN. Yeah! That's what I'm talking about. That's right.

TRUSS. Ryan, he gets one cap.

RYAN. Huh? One cap!? Why? That's not fair.

TRUSS. No, it's not.

SABINA. You said I'd be forgiven.

TRUSS. And you are, but you still have to pay for what you did.

SABINA. Where the fuck do you get off? You took Oakley's gun!

TRUSS. So?

SABINA. So? He took a gun.

TRUSS. For us. To protect us. You think they're holding out on each other out there? They're a well-oiled team, watching each other's back without question. That's how they're beating us. We have to use every-thing we got to beat them back. I mean, am I alone in here? Cuz I'm starting to think I'm the only one who gives a shit.

RYAN. I want two caps! I demand two caps!

FELIZ. I'll give you one of mine.

TRUSS. You can't do that.

FELIZ. You said I get two capfuls of water. They're mine to do with as I please, and I decided to give one of mine to Ryan. There's nothing you can say about it.

RYAN. Right. There's nothing you can say about it. You can't keep water from me!

SABINA. Oh, shut up. At least you get water.

RYAN. You had half the fucking bottle already.

SABINA. But he took his gun!

TRUSS. *(To FELIZ.)* Fine. Give him your share, but don't come complaining to me in a few hours.

FELIZ. You won't have to worry about that.

TRUSS. No one eats the gum or the...Sour Puss...things...unless it's an emergency. That shit'll only make you more thirsty and we'll crash from the sugar if we're not careful. *(TRUSS locks the candy in the box. He keeps one key and gives the other to FELIZ.)* Hold onto this. We need both keys to open this box, right?

FELIZ. That's right.

TRUSS. When you're done passing out the water, it gets locked back up 'til the next hour. *(TRUSS looks at SABINA.)* You don't have any more "snacking places," do you?

SABINA. Kiss my ass!

TRUSS. You can kiss mine when we get out of here alive.

RYAN. I'm ready for my water now.

(Lights fade.

Lights up. More time has passed. Everyone is sweating heavily from the hours of heat taking its toll. FELIZ is organizing items in the safe with an eerie calm. SABINA and RYAN sit in close proximity, drained.)

RYAN. Sabina.

SABINA. What?

RYAN. *(Lowering his voice.)* Look, you and I got off-track somewhere.

SABINA. Was it when you wanted Truss to lock me up instead of you?

RYAN. What? No.

SABINA. Was it when you thought it was funny I didn't get any water?

RYAN. I'm sorry. Okay? It was the heat.

(Pause.)

SABINA. Was it when you didn't want to admit you hit on me?

RYAN. I'm really sorry about all that. Listen--

SABINA. Why? So you can lie to me again?

RYAN. No. *(RYAN motions for SABINA to come closer. SABINA looks back to TRUSS, who is making noise, rummaging around, not paying any attention to them. She moves close to RYAN and looks at him to continue.)* I think you and I can help each other.

SABINA. How?

RYAN. Get me out of these.

SABINA. Why should I?

RYAN. Because he's gonna kill me if you don't.

SABINA. He might kill me if I do.

RYAN. Has it ever occurred to you that Truss, as a hostage, has now *taken* a hostage? Do you find any irony in that?

SABINA. I don't have time for irony. I am hot, sweaty, and so thirsty I've thought about drinking my own piss. I'm also really claustrophobic and have nightmares of being shot in the head. So, if you think I'm dealing with this situation poorly, tough shit.

RYAN. Okay, I'm sorry. You're right. It's not your problem. *(RYAN changes gears.)* I didn't know you had nightmares about stuff like that.

(SABINA pauses for a moment, trying to read RYAN'S intentions.)

SABINA. Ever since I was a little girl.

RYAN. That's rough.

SABINA. *(Defensive)* Yes, it is. *(RYAN looks on sympathetically, nodding. SABINA relaxes.)* All kinds of nightmares. Being buried alive, drowning or getting shot. Blood. There's always blood in the dreams.

RYAN. Really?

(SABINA nods, completely engrossed.)

SABINA. So many bad dreams, so much blood...I stared thinking maybe my fears were really premonitions. A sixth sense of how I'm going to die.

RYAN. Interesting.

(SABINA looks at RYAN, immediately suspicious. The earnestness on his face causes her to relax once again.)

SABINA. So...do you have any paralyzing fears?

RYAN. What?

SABINA. You know, like, things that haunt you. Premonitions of how you're going to die?

RYAN. Oh...yeah. Sure, but not being shot or suffocated.

SABINA. What, then?

RYAN. Well, I've always been scared of...no nevermind.

SABINA. What? What are you scared of?

RYAN. No, it's stupid.
SABINA. Come on. I just told you mine.

(Pause)

RYAN. Puppets.
SABINA. Puppets?
RYAN. Ventriloquists' dummies, animatronic creatures, umm...wax statues, basically anything that falsely represents a living thing.
SABINA. Automatonophobia.
RYAN. There's a name for it?
SABINA. You'd be surprised at how many names there are for things like that.
RYAN. I thought I was the only one.
SABINA. You think puppets are going to kill you?
RYAN. On my fifth birthday, my folks threw a big party. They were having problems, and I guess they felt they could make it up to me with clowns, ponies, and ice cream cake. The main event was Freddy and Pickles, a ventriloquist act. Pickles was his dummy and he dressed him like a...a Hasidic Jew. You know with the black hat and coat. He even had the curly hair twirling down the side of his little hat. I was mesmerized. To me, Pickles was as real as any other kid, and he made me laugh. So I took him. I waited 'til they finished the act, and while Freddy was getting some cake, I popped open his box and hid the little Jewish puppet in my room. I had him for weeks. I brought him food and water, but he never touched it. I thought it was part of his religion. We had a great time. Then one day I decided we'd go play in the yard. It was Sunday, so I thought it would be okay, it being God's day and all. I loved to create little make-believe scenarios, like Lost in the Jungle, Space Planet Seven, or sometimes I'd just take off his pants and dance him around. My mom called me in for lunch from the house. She didn't know about Pickles, so my plan was to leave him in the tall grass and when I was done with lunch go back outside, get him, and sneak him back to my room. I was halfway through my jelly sandwich when I heard the lawn mower. I froze. If I made a move and ran for him, the gig would be up, and if I stayed and finished my sandwich, Pickles

would die.

SABINA. What did you do? *(RYAN'S look says it all.)* You ate the rest of your sandwich.

RYAN. It took me like three days to find all of him. A wood chip here. A wood chip there. A little curl of hair.

SABINA. You must have been devastated?

RYAN. Well, yeah, I killed my best friend. Then, on my sixth birthday, my parents took me to a puppet show. I took one look at that little stage, saw the shadow of a puppet just behind the little curtain, and freaked out. I couldn't stop shaking. I was terrified one of those little fuckers was going to exact their revenge for Pickles by strangling me with the wires they hang from. To this day, I can't...you know, go to theme parks or wax museums. I know now they're not real, but I believe in karma, and the fear of one of them going haywire and killing me still comes up.

SABINA. That's by far the most fucked up thing I've heard in a long time.

RYAN. It's ridiculous, I know, but I'm convinced I will die at the hands of some type of puppet!

SABINA. Puppets.

RYAN. I guess we both have a psychic sense of things.

(Pause. SABINA and RYAN seem to be getting more comfortable with each other.)

SABINA. You know, I saw a video article on premonitions a while back. JFK had nightmares of being shot in the head. So did Abe Lincoln and Kurt Cobain.

RYAN. Kurt Cobain shot himself.

SABINA. *(Conspiratorially)* Did he?

RYAN. Yah. They found him dead with the shotgun and a suicide note.

SABINA. Right. And I suppose black helicopters, chem-trails, and the illuminati don't exist. Why don't we learn? Every time some cover-up gets declassified we shrug our shoulders and say, "Wow, that's crazy." Yet, it's like pulling teeth to get anyone to believe that same shit

is happening right now. I don't know if aliens exist, but I know conspir-
acies do.

RYAN. I never thought of it that way. You're a smart woman.

SABINA. What's that supposed to mean?

RYAN. Nothing. Just the way he treats you. I think he doesn't give
you enough credit.

SABINA. Who? Truss?

RYAN. I don't want to start something. I shouldn't have said anything.

SABINA. You think I don't know what kind of guy he is?

RYAN. I'm sure you do. You're not stupid. You see he's a murderer
and a tyrant. I just don't know why you let him treat you like that.

SABINA. I know what I'm doing. I know exactly what I'm doing.
So don't flatter yourself. Don't try and be my hero and get all chivalrous.

RYAN. I'm not. I just think you're smarter than him. I'm sure you
realize he's using you.

(Pause)

SABINA. Of course I do.

RYAN. Right. I'm agreeing with you. I mean, it sucks being made
an example of. Doesn't it? *(An awkward moment, then...)* Look, I'm still
locked up here.

SABINA. I don't have the key. Truss does.

RYAN. Uh-huh. Can you get it from him before I end up like
Oakley?

SABINA, What am I gonna do? Bang him over the head?

RYAN. Why not?

*(TRUSS, who's been working on something, lifts a crude object into the
air, made of various articles from the safe and OAKLEY'S personal
effects.)*

TRUSS. This'll take somebody's head clear off!

SABINA. I'll give you some of my candy bar.

RYAN. No thanks.

SABINA. It's okay. He said I could share it.

RYAN. I don't need a snack. I need to get loose.

SABINA. You sure? It's an Oh Henry.

RYAN. No thank you. Why don't you give it to Truss? I'm sure he could use the strength when he pulls the trigger.

SABINA. Fine, but he didn't want it. He's allergic.

RYAN. Allergic?

SABINA. Something to do with nuts.

(SABINA walks off.)

RYAN. Wait. Sabina. *(SABINA stops.)* You know what? I'll take a piece for later.

SABINA. Sure.

(SABINA breaks off some of the candy bar and puts it in RYAN'S shirt pocket.)

TRUSS. Time.

(Everyone looks up as TRUSS, checking his watch, steps to the water box. FELIZ, who has been busy, tidying up the safe, making notes, and generally preparing for something, stops and calmly walks over to TRUSS. They both use their respective keys and remove a dangerously low water bottle from the safety deposit box. TRUSS pours two caps and drinks, then passes the bottle to FELIZ. She pours one cap, drinks, and walks over to RYAN and SABINA. There is something lost about her.)

SABINA. I can't watch this.

(SABINA starts to walk away.)

RYAN. Sabina?

SABINA. Yeah?

RYAN. Eventually, I'm going to get out of these things. *(SABINA goes. FELIZ arrives with the bottle, kneels and begins to pour a cap for RYAN.)* Oh, I got her. She's stuck blinking twelve, that one. *(FELIZ lifts the cap to RYAN'S mouth. He drinks. FELIZ starts to pour another.)* It's only a matter of time now. Listen, here's my plan. I don't know when or how she's going to get me out of these, but when she does...*(FELIZ is unaware she's tipping the cap to one side, letting water spill out on the floor. She stares off into the distance.)* Jesus! Feliz, what are you doing?

FELIZ. What?

RYAN. The cap. The cap!

FELIZ. *(Indifferent)* Oh. I'm sorry. I wasn't paying attention.

RYAN. I only got one cap. Shit. What's wrong with you? You've been like a zombie, moving shit around, talking nonsense. Wake up! I get a do-over; that was a miss. I get another cap.

(FELIZ begins to fill another cap. TRUSS sees this and marches over.)

TRUSS. What do you think you're doing?

RYAN. Hurry up, he's coming. *(TRUSS takes the water and cap from FELIZ before RYAN gets it to his lips.)* Oh...come on, man. It was a miss.

TRUSS. I don't care what it was. I said two caps, not three.

RYAN. She spilt one on the floor. I should get another.

TRUSS. Two. I don't care if one of them is on the floor. Two caps were poured from this bottle.

RYAN. It wasn't my fault. She wasn't paying attention, and it...you know, tipped. Something is wrong with her. Staring off into space like a junkie half the time. *(TRUSS, who has been looking at the floor, bends down and picks up the log book. He begins to skim through the pages.)* Writing in that book. Moving things around.

FELIZ. That book is none of your business.

TRUSS. Why?

FELIZ. Put it down. It's personal.

TRUSS. It's the safe's log book. How is that personal?

FELIZ. I...I've been writing to my husband.

TRUSS. Oh...him.

FELIZ. Personal things. In case we don't make it out of here.

(TRUSS Stops on one page in particular. He begins to read with great interest.) Give me back my book!

(FELIZ makes a move for the book.)

TRUSS. Wait a minute. What is this?
RYAN. What?
TRUSS. Oh this is rich!
RYAN. What?
TRUSS. Do you normally write to dead people?
RYAN. What does that mean?
TRUSS. Do you want me to tell them or should I?

(FELIZ looks at the group, studying them; finally, she speaks.)

FELIZ. My husband passed away a few years ago.
SABINA. He's dead? How was he gonna call the police? *(Everyone looks at SABINA.)* Oh, right. You bitch!
TRUSS. It gets better. *(TRUSS begins reading from the log book.)* "We killed Oakley. Truss strangled him while the rest of us just watched."
SABINA. What?!
TRUSS. Not only did bank manager here give you all a false sense of hope but she's written a dying declaration to her dead hubby implicating all of us in Oakley's murder.
RYAN. Whoa...you guys, not me.
FELIZ. Yes, you! We all took a life!
SABINA. Have you lost your mind?
TRUSS. What happened in this safe stays here.
FELIZ. People have to know.
TRUSS. We did what we did so we could get out of here.
FELIZ. And if we do, then what? Go home? Get something to eat? Take a shower?
TRUSS. According to you, we're all supposed to go directly to jail.
SABINA. All I did was show up for work today. I'm not going to jail for that dead motherfucker!

TRUSS. He was a threat to all of us! Plain and simple. Can't you see that?

FELIZ. You know what I see when I look at him laying there? I don't see a sixty-year-old, down-on-his-luck security guard. I see the expression on his parents' faces the day they brought him home from the hospital. The look of not wanting anything in the world to ever hurt him. Now look at him. Look at him, and tell me that wasn't a precious life. How can any of you live with the knowledge of what we did?

TRUSS. I'll live with the evidence of four lives saved by killing one.

FELIZ. I wish I could do that.

SABINA. We have to get rid of her...I mean this.

TRUSS. Hold on, let's see what else she wrote first? *(TRUSS reads more from the log. His eyes widen.)* You have got to be kidding me! *(TRUSS raises the log book as if he may strike FELIZ with it. He stops himself.)* I could kill you!

FELIZ. You don't scare me anymore.

SABINA. What now?

TRUSS. How long have you known about this?

RYAN. Known about what?

FELIZ. I'm cleaning up.

(FELIZ goes back to her business.)

TRUSS. How much time do we have left?

RYAN. Why?

TRUSS. Because we're running out of air.

RYAN. What?

TRUSS. She also lied to us about how much air we have.

RYAN. You said we'd be fine!

FELIZ. For a few hours.

RYAN. That's not what you said, Feliz!

SABINA. I knew it! Didn't I tell you? But no. No one listens to me!

FELIZ. I didn't know we would be in here this long. I didn't know we'd murder someone.

RYAN. You lied?

FELIZ. I didn't lie.

RYAN. Everything you said is a lie!

FELIZ. I told you what I knew at the time. To keep everyone calm.

RYAN. Don't get fucking rhetorical!

FELIZ. Okay.

RYAN. Why would you lie to us about how much air we have?

FELIZ. There was enough air in this safe for a few hours. That's how long I thought we'd be in here.

RYAN. Don't you think you should have said something before?

TRUSS. How much time do we have left?

FELIZ. I thought this would all be over by now. I didn't want to alarm anyone.

RYAN. What were you gonna do, wait 'til we drop dead, then mention it?

SABINA. Yeah? What were you gonna do?

TRUSS. How much time!?

FELIZ. I can't be sure exactly.

SABINA. We might as well be in a fuckin' coffin!

TRUSS. Give or take?

FELIZ. One of our tellers was locked in a few years ago. I got the feeling it was important they get him out quickly.

SABINA. I knew I was going to die in here.

TRUSS. What else are you lying about?

FELIZ. I never thought it would come to this, but it has. I thought they'd leave, but then they...I don't know. Then I figured my husband...well, we needed hope. Didn't we? I thought someone, anyone would call the police and they would show up and let us out. None of that happened. And now, after everything...after how we've behaved, I'm not so sure it should.

(Everyone lets the this information sink in.)

TRUSS. As soon as anyone feels light-headed, speak up. We won't have much time from that point on.

SABINA. I feel light-headed. I can smell the air getting thinner already.

FELIZ. Please, God, let her pass out first.

SABINA. We wouldn't be here if you'd hit the alarm.

FELIZ. Me?

SABINA. And you gave out the code!

FELIZ. It's protocol. Do what they want and get them out before anyone gets hurt.

SABINA. I'd say collapsing because you can't very well breathe is going to hurt. It's going to hurt pretty bad, Feliz!

FELIZ. I can't wait. Then I won't have to hear your incessant whining.

SABINA. You're old!

FELIZ. Or they could come in and drag you away to the *sodomy* room.

RYAN. At least Sabina never lied to us.

SABINA. Thank you.

FELIZ. Oh, please. Didn't you just tell me she was stupid?

SABINA. What?

RYAN. I did not.

FELIZ. "I got her." Isn't that what you said? What did you mean by that?

SABINA. "Got" me?

RYAN. Wow, you just keep lying. You can't stop.

SABINA. You made up Mr. Pickles?

RYAN. You're listening to her? She's crazy. She probably still sets a plate and talks to an empty chair at dinner every night.

FELIZ. It doesn't matter. We won't last 'til Monday. Excuse me, there's a lot to be done.

(This stops everyone cold.)

TRUSS. She's right.

RYAN. Whoa...hold on. That's it? Do some house work while we wait for the air to go?

TRUSS. We overestimated them. Unfortunately I don't think they have a clue! If they did we would've been used for leverage against their demands. No one's even come in here.

RYAN. And that's a bad thing?

TRUSS. If no one comes in, getting the jump on them and escaping is moot. It's different now. Bank manager here fixed it so we don't have a whole lot of time left to figure things out. But we need to get them to open the door so we can breathe.

SABINA. And how do you suggest we do that?

(TRUSS is thinking hard. The weight of what he's about to say is troubling.)

TRUSS. I didn't want to resort to this.

SABINA. Resort to what?

TRUSS. I thought about this earlier but...well...there is something we can do. We can compromise the one thing they came here to get and won't leave without. *(Everyone cocks their heads, their interest piqued.)* The money! They're too far into this to leave without the majority of their score.

SABINA. I don't follow you.

(TRUSS pulls a lighter from his pocket.)

TRUSS. We torch it.

(Pause, TRUSS nods his head, as the group processes what he just said.)

RYAN. You want to set a fire in here?

TRUSS. Yeah.

RYAN. You're certifiable!

TRUSS. It's extreme, but it makes perfect sense. They'll bust in here, for sure.

RYAN. And if they don't, we burn to death. Great plan, Captain Quick.

(TRUSS marches towards RYAN.)

TRUSS. How about I kick you in the teeth?! How's that for a plan?

(TRUSS feigns kicking RYAN. RYAN flinches.) **One more time, fucker. Test me one more time.**

SABINA. No! I'm not going to burn to death. No way I'm going out like that!

TRUSS. That's not gonna happen. We'll have them face down begging for a quick death by the time the fire's a factor. It's only two of them, for Christ's sake. Maybe three. We can do this. We can take them out ourselves!

SABINA. I thought the idea was to keep those guys away from us?

TRUSS. Somebody needs to come through that door in order for us to get out of here. I'm just speeding up the process.

SABINA. You can't do that.

TRUSS. The money's federally insured, if that's what you're concerned about.

SABINA. This is an air-tight vault. Either way, we'll choke to death.

TRUSS. If we stay low, air won't be a problem. I guarantee that door opens the minute they realize their money's on fire.

RYAN. And how are they going to know the money is on fire?

SABINA. Yeah.

TRUSS. The video camera on the wall.

SABINA. You're making a lot of assumptions. What if they're not even watching the monitors?

TRUSS. Well...

SABINA. "Well," what?

TRUSS. We die.

SABINA. That's it?

FELIZ. Let's do it.

SABINA. Don't listen to her. She wants to die.

TRUSS. That's it. I didn't want to do it this way, but we either suffocate waiting, or roll the dice and get out of here now. Me, I'd rather die trying.

SABINA. I'd rather not die at all.

TRUSS No one wants that, but we have to be realistic. There is a finite amount of air left. Once it's gone, so are we. None of us have the option to wait any longer.

SABINA. How could this happen?

TRUSS. Life is a series of subtractions.

(Pause)

SABINA. If no one comes...will it hurt?
TRUSS. We'll pass out from the smoke before our bodies start burning.
SABINA. Oh, God!
TRUSS. I know what I'm asking, so I won't do this without everyone agreeing. But the way I see it, we don't have a choice. At least my way offers some hope of getting out alive. *(TRUSS looks everyone in the eye.)* We can do this!

(Long pause.)

FELIZ. I'll agree.
TRUSS. You?
SABINA. I don't know.
TRUSS. Sabina, I know you're scared, but you have to be brave.
SABINA. But I'm not.
TRUSS. Then pretend.
SABINA. Okay.

(Everyone looks at RYAN, who's been thinking hard.)

TRUSS. Ryan?
RYAN. Yeah.
TRUSS. "Yeah," what?
RYAN. Okay, I'm in. Under one condition.
TRUSS. What?
RYAN. You let me out of these.
TRUSS. I don't know.
RYAN. I'm totally restricted. What if they come in here and there's a struggle? I've got more gun training than you. I can watch your back.
TRUSS. You mean stab it.
RYAN. I hate you, I'm not trying to hide that. But my desire to get

out of this safe supersedes everything.

TRUSS. I'm sorry, but I can't take that risk.

RYAN. Then I take back my vote.

TRUSS. Too late. You already cast it.

RYAN. Bullshit!

TRUSS. We know where you stand. You've spoken; you can't take that back.

RYAN. Fine.

TRUSS. *(To SABINA.)* Help me move the money to a better spot. *(TRUSS turns to FELIZ.)* Pull that chair under the video camera. Now, I don't know how much of us they've been watching, but we're gonna give them a perfect view of their riches going up in smoke. Aim the camera at that corner. Make sure you can't see the opposite side of the door. That's where I'll be hiding when they come in. *(Everyone, except RYAN, puts TRUSS' plan into action.)* When I'm set, one of you will light the fire and get out of the way. I have six shots; that leaves three bullets per bad guy. Two if there's three of them. Pretty good odds I'll hit them all, but if I don't, make sure that mace is ready.

RYAN. You're not going to set that pile of money on fire.

TRUSS. You've had your say already.

RYAN. You won't be able to do it.

TRUSS. Why?

RYAN. Those bills are packed too tight. It's like trying to set a huge log on fire with a match. It's too dense.

(TRUSS thinks for a moment.)

FELIZ. He's right. We should pull them out of the straps and spread them out.

TRUSS. Make a pile. Good call.

RYAN. No problem.

(FELIZ and SABINA begin tearing the bricks of money apart and tossing them into a pile. TRUSS walks over to RYAN.)

TRUSS. If something goes wrong when they come in, can you fight better than you did before?

RYAN. Hey, I was going easy on you. I wrestled in high school.

TRUSS. I knew there was something gay about you.

(Both men share a laugh and with that TRUSS reaches behind RYAN'S back and unlocks his cuffs.)

RYAN. Thanks.

(TRUSS turns to walk back to FELIZ and SABINA. With the fiercest of speed, RYAN bum rushes TRUSS, lowers his shoulder, and with a devastating blow, knocks TRUSS down. The two men struggle, but it is RYAN who comes up with the gun. As if on cue, SABINA darts to safety in the shadows of the safe. Out of breath, RYAN levels the barrel at TRUSS' head.)

RYAN. I told you, you better hope I never get out of these.

FELIZ. What are you doing?

RYAN. Shut up!

SABINA. *(From the darkness.)* Ryan. Are you serious?

RYAN. Put these on.

(RYAN hands TRUSS the handcuffs.)

TRUSS. No.

RYAN. I said put them on. *(RYAN forces TRUSS into the handcuffs.)* Do all of you really want to commit suicide?

TRUSS. Not suicide. A way out.

RYAN. Like Jonestown, you sadistic fuck?

TRUSS. You're gonna hurt yourself with that.

RYAN. Just you.

TRUSS. Put the gun down, Ryan.

FELIZ. Let him set the fire.

(RYAN levels the gun on FELIZ.)

RYAN. Don't you even start with me. If I had another set of those, you'd be right next to him. All three of you.

SABINA. Them, not me. Not me, Ryan.

TRUSS. Calm down. We can talk this through.

RYAN. Now you want to talk? You didn't want to talk it through when I was tied to a pole and left for bait. No one helped me. No one's rational side came out then. Now you want me to calm down?

TRUSS. You're not thinking straight.

RYAN. Maybe it's the lack of oxygen to my brain. You think that could be it?

SABINA. Ryan, I didn't want to do this, and I don't know why Truss wanted you locked up.

TRUSS. You know damn well why I locked him up. Hell, you helped me pin him down.

RYAN. That's right. But you know what? I'm not upset with you, Sabina. You're too dumb to be angry at. You don't know any better.

SABINA. That's right.

(RYAN points the gun again at TRUSS.)

RYAN. How does it feel? You're right. It feels good to take things into your own hands.

TRUSS. What are you gonna do now?

(RYAN pulls out half of the candy bar SABINA gave him.)

RYAN. Eat it.

TRUSS. *(To SABINA.)* Oh, you conniving bitch.

RYAN. Eat it.

TRUSS. I can't eat that.

RYAN. Eat it!

TRUSS. I'll go into anaphylactic shock. Without my meds, I'll die in less than twenty minutes. But I'm sure you know that already.

RYAN. I guess you have a choice to make. Eat it, and take the chance we get out of here in time for your medication, or don't, and I shoot you in the head. I think you should eat it. After all, you said you'd rather die trying.

TRUSS. You wouldn't shoot me. You don't have the balls.

RYAN. Well, you know what they say about people held in captivity? They adapt. *(RYAN pistol whips TRUSS.)* Now eat it!

(TRUSS stares coldly at RYAN, blood dripping down the side of his face. It's obvious TRUSS won't budge. RYAN breaks off a piece of the candy bar and, with his free hand, squeezes TRUSS' face, forcing his mouth open. It's an awkward struggle, but inevitably, RYAN violently drives the chocolate bar into TRUSS' mouth.)

RYAN. Good. That is a damn fine candy bar, isn't it? And it's Job, Truss...in the Bible, the one who waited and waited...*(TRUSS defiantly bites down into RYAN'S hand. RYAN pulls back.)* Ahhh! FUCK! *(TRUSS spits out what's left in his mouth, but the damage has already been done. RYAN regroups, shaking out the pain.)* Did you think I didn't see what you were up to? Do you think I was just gonna let you set us all on fire? What...you think because I have money, that makes me stupid or weak? Well, I'm not! It doesn't! *(RYAN kicks TRUSS.)* You want to know what's wrong with the world, Truss? Assumptions. Not apathy. Not money. Assumptions. I've spent half my life trying to dodge them. I went to a goddamn art school and pissed my father's money away so I could draw a perfect circle. Freehand. And I hate art! I fucking hate it, but in the end it didn't matter. They all assumed I was a tool because my family didn't have to kill themselves for a living. *(RYAN seems possessed now.)* And you're no fucking different, Truss! You turned every unknown into the worst situation you could imagine. Your assumptions led us to kill a man and pick through his stuff. You held me hostage and became a savage.

TRUSS. And I suppose you had nothing to do with it?

RYAN. No! You took away my free will.

TRUSS. You made a choice every step of the way. All of you.

RYAN. You're poison. Tapping on the wall does not mean a SWAT team. Random noises, lights going out do not mean Armageddon. You've assumed things you had no right to. And the rest of you let him. You are all just the same as him! Until they walk through that door, we're alone, otherwise we've assumed they're here for no reason. We assumed Oakley was a threat. We've assumed Truss knew what he was saying and doing. We assumed your husband called the police.

SABINA. *(Stepping out of the shadows.)* We assumed the door was locked.

RYAN. All of that stops, now!!

FELIZ. The safe door. We've assumed it's locked.

RYAN. Don't start with me.

FELIZ. All this time. No one checked.

RYAN. I have the gun.

SABINA. Ryan, check the door.

(Long pause. No one wants to check it out. Finally, SABINA moves towards the door.)

FELIZ. No. Don't.

(SABINA arrives at the safe door and opens it, revealing that it has been unlocked all this time. She runs out to see. After a moment she comes back. The look on her face says it all. Silence and then, as the lights fade, the intermittent sounds of TRUSS beginning to desperately gasp for air.)

LIGHTS OUT. END OF PLAY.

SAFE

PROP LIST

SET	ITEM	NOTES

Act I

ON STAGE

SET	ITEM	NOTES
UL	Money (10)	*Scattered at random on floor*
	Gold necklace with oval centerpiece	
	Black oval pin with	
	Gold hoops (2)	
	Safety box w/o red ties	*On top of next safety box*
	Safety box with red ties	
	Pearl Necklaces (3)	*Hanging from open deposit box*
SL	Stacks of money (4)	*By pole*
	Money (4-6)	*Scattered below safe*
DL	Money (10)	*Scattered at random on floor*
	Gold chain	
	Certificates (3 rolled / 3 loose)	
	SAFE	
	Stacks of money (15-25)	*Dispersed evenly in safe*
	Money (3-5)	*Hanging out of safe*
UR	Money (18)	*Scattered randomly on floor*
	Gold Chain	
DR	Money (7)	
	Gold chain (UL corner of table)	
	Heart jewelry	
	Gold hoops (3)	
	TABLE	

SET	ITEM	NOTES

Log book *(UL corner of table)*
Pen   *Linked onto log book*
LARGE SAFETY DEPOSIT BOX
Certificates (2)
Heart jewelry

OFF SL
Money (12)
Mace
Pencil
Dummy legs

PRE SET SR SAFETY DEPOSIT BOX 1975
Bottled water (2)   *One bottle dangerously low*
Sour patch kids
Zip lock bag filled w/ gum balls
Twinkie wrapper

CHK: Ryan and Feliz
Cell phone (2)

CHK: Oakley
Gun   *With ankle straps*
(wardrobe) Cop belt

SET	ITEM	NOTES

Act II, Scene 1

ON STAGE

UL   Money (10)   *Scattered at random on floor*
Gold necklace with oval centerpiece
Black oval pin with
Gold hoops (2)

SET	ITEM	NOTES
	Safety box w/o red ties	
	Safety box with red ties	*On top of other safety box*
	Pearl Necklaces (3)	*Hanging from open deposit box*
SL	Stacks of money (4)	*By pole*
	Money (4-6)	*Scattered below safe*
DL	Money (10)	*Scattered at random on floor*
	Gold chain	
	Certificates (3 rolled / 3 loose)	
	Chair	*Up against wall*
	SAFE	
	Stacks of money (15-25)	*Dispersed evenly in safe*
	Money (3?5)	*Hanging out of safe*
UR	Money (30)	*Scattered randomly on floor*
	Gold Chain	
	Pencil	
	Chair	*Angled towards door*
DR	Money (7)	
	Gold Chain *(UR corner of table)*	
	Heart Jewelry	
	Log Book	*Between table and chair*
	Gold Hoops (3)	
	Mace *(UR inside corner of table)*	

Personal: RYAN
      Handcuffs
Personal: OAKLEY
(wardrobe) Shoelaces/Cop Belt
Personal: SABINA
      Oh Henry Bar (2)   *One Oh Henry half eaten*
Personal: TRUSS
      Gun/Lighter

SOUND CUES

All CUES listed below are called by Stage Manager.
NOTE: All music in original production of SAFE was written and
composed by Mark Bruckner, Misha Lepetich and Anthony Ruvivar

Act I		**Notes**
	SQ A Pre Show Music	*Prior to house opening*
Pg 1	SQ B Pre show out / top of the show music go	
Pg 1	SQ C Looping (1:15) top of the show music fade slightly	
Pg 2	SQ C.1 Top of the show out at fucking kill you	
Pg 54	SQ D After Feliz Oh my God!	

INTERMISSION (15 min.)

Act II		**Notes**
	SQ E Top of Act II	
Pg 64	SQ F Sound EFX on Feliz … do if you	
Pg 71	SQ G End of Act II:i	
Pg 80	SQ H And of Act II:ii	
Pg 80	SQ H.1 0:15 fade out	
Pg 107	SQ I Curtain call	*0:10 seconds into BO*

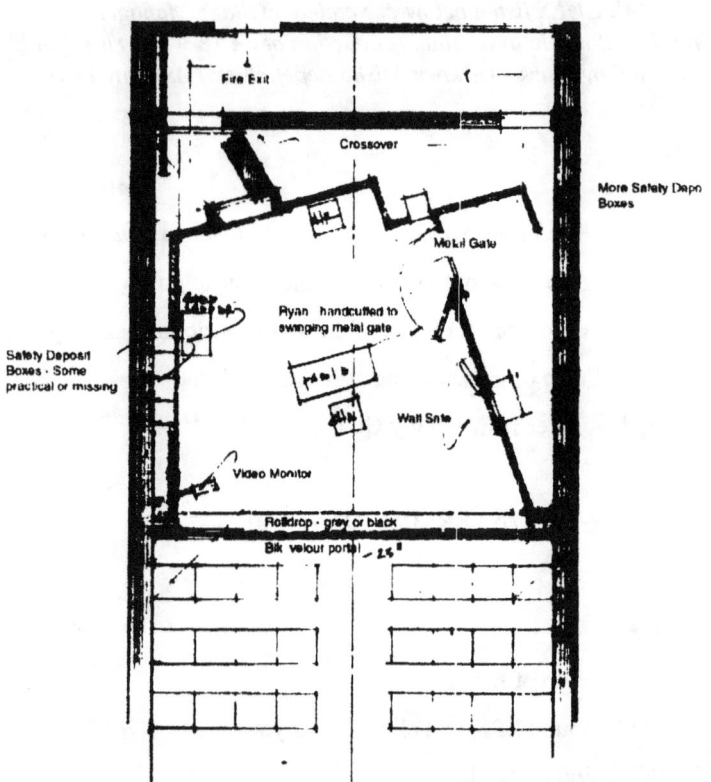

Safe   **Preliminary Groundplan #2   1/4" = 1'-0"**

THE OFFICE PLAYS
Two full length plays by Adam Bock

THE RECEPTIONIST
Comedy / 2m., 2f. Interior

At the start of a typical day in the Northeast Office, Beverly deals effortlessly with ringing phones and her colleague's romantic troubles. But the appearance of a charming rep from the Central Office disrupts the friendly routine. And as the true nature of the company's business becomes apparent, The Receptionist raises disquieting, provocative questions about the consequences of complicity with evil.

"...Mr. Bock's poisoned Post-it note of a play."
- New York Times

"Bock's intense initial focus on the routine goes to the heart of *The Receptionist's* pointed, painfully timely allegory... elliptical, provocative play..."
- Time Out New York

THE THUGS
Comedy / 2m, 6f / Interior

The Obie Award winning dark comedy about work, thunder and the mysterious things that are happening on the 9th floor of a big law firm. When a group of temps try to discover the secrets that lurk in the hidden crevices of their workplace, they realize they would rather believe in gossip and rumors than face dangerous realities.

"Bock starts you off giggling, but leaves you with a chill."
- Time Out New York

"... a delightfully paranoid little nightmare that is both more chillingly realistic and pointedly absurd than anything John Grisham ever dreamed up."
- New York Times